J. L. F

MURDER
ON THE
ENGLISH RIVIERA

O'NEILL PUBLISHING

PUBLISHED BY
O'NEILL PUBLISHERS 1995
BIRMINGHAM

J. L. HARWARD 1994

Printed by Baker Bond Printers, Brownhills

CHAPTERS

FOREWARD

My love of Devon, and especially Torquay where I spent my childhood holidays, and also a fascination of the murder mystery has inspired me to write this book.

I hope you get as much enjoyment out of reading this novel as I have writing it.

CHAPTER ONE

A New beginning

As she looked out over the still Torbay Sea on that lovely September morning, Rosemary felt at peace. Her state of mind was as tranquil and serene as the view before her. This was a feeling she had often encountered since moving to Devon, the place she had loved as a child, and where she had hoped to spend the rest of her days. Quite a few days in fact, as she was only in her early forties!

She had finally left the hustle and bustle of the Midlands behind her, although Torquay could be hectic in the height of the summer, at this time of year, with less visitors, and those mostly pensioners. Rosemary found it idyllic. Feeling as she did at that moment in time, she could never have envisaged this new found happiness was to be short-lived, and the turmoil and trouble that was to beset her over the next few weeks.

The events that were to follow would throw her life and the lives of those around her into complete chaos.

It was undoubtedly a big decision that she and her husband George had to make; leaving both their jobs, selling the house where their daughter had been born, and parting from dear family and friends.

They could not have done it when Sarah was younger, she was quite adamant she wouldn't leave her school friends, but now she was at university, and only came home at term time, it was not a problem, in fact she now thought it was quite a novelty coming home to the seaside.

George still had his doubts, about taking on the running of a hotel, with all the risks involved, and Rosemary was more apprehensive than she liked to admit, even though she had loved Torquay as a child when she had spent her summer holidays there. The place for her had never lost it's charm and excitement, as so many things often do as the years go by.

But she was now middle-aged with all the pressures and responsibilities that come with time.

She wouldn't be holidaying there any more, she would be living there and doing her utmost to survive in a business she didn't know that much about.

Any doubts they did have seem to fade into oblivion, when they first set their eyes on the Sherwell Hotel. They were totally enraptured by the place, and Rosemary was hardly paying any attention to the estate agent as he went from room to room with his clipboard and sales jargon. He said how the previous owners had made it a thriving business and were forced to sell due to the husband's ill health.

The hotel was situated in Chelston, not far from Torquay station. Chelston had lots of charm, though quite hilly, but because the hotel was at the top of a hill, the sea views were magnificent. It had a character all of its own. It was a double fronted Victoria style residence set in about an acre of ground, built in red brick with tall, impressive bay windows either side of the front door.

The entrance was charming. There was a large oak door with Terracotta urns, either side filled with an array of shrubs and flowers.

The front garden consisted of a half-moon shaped gravel drive with a small lawn and rockery, in the centre, and it was all set behind a brick wall, that was just high enough for privacy, without spoiling the look of the house.

There was no doubt it was just what they'd been looking for so they put in an offer, waited anxiously for a few days, and then had welcome news that it had been accepted. So after several nailbiting weeks, of mortgage arrangements, surveys and solicitors the Sherwell Hotel was finally theirs.

They moved in April and after about six months they were getting on their feet. Things were finally coming together and business was fairly good.

They had acquired a cook, Lil, who was a bit of a grumpy old soul, but they could put up with that because her cooking was beyond compare – her steak and kidney pie was the talking point of most of the guests.

The gardener, Tom, had been inherited from the last owners. He was retired and did a few hours a week, and any odd jobs that needed doing.

The only other staff they could afford to employ was Mary, a young Irish girl. She was a little scatterbrained at times, but not a bad worker.

The rest of the chores, George and Rosemary shared between them. They waited on tables, ran the bar, did the reception work – there weren't enough hours in the day!!

They had been too busy to be home-sick but had missed their friends, 'The old gang back home' as George affectionately called them. So, after several days of telephoning and arranging, Rosemary managed to get them all to come and stay, when they were fairly quiet. She had made it quite clear, they would all have to pay, although she had given them a reduced rate, they were not in a position financially to have them as their guests.

CHAPTER TWO

The old gang arrive

'Why on earth have you brought that extra case, Mavis?' Simon asked, fidgeting on his seat.

'Well dear, with your waterproofs and wellingtons, there wasn't much room for my clothes!'

'Nonsense, you women are all the same, you take far too many clothes on holiday . . . and that one dress you bought was a wicked waste of money!' Simon said vehemently. 'You know I had to get those new rods and floats, I intend to do some fishing and I needed that book on seafishing and you friviously go and buy a new dress.'

Simon took up three seats on the train. He was surrounded by various fishing paraphernalia, books and magazines. He had on his wax jacket, even though it was a warm day.

'Be a love and go and get me a couple of ham rolls from the buffet car, will you, Mavis?'

He took a quick swig of whisky from his pocket

flask.

'Do you really need to drink that on the journey?'

'You know I always take whisky on the river bank, it can get cold.'

'Yes' implored Mavis, 'but it must be at least seventy degrees in this carriage!'

'Now dear, don't be a nag. We'll be there soon and you can have some nice long chats with Rosemary and catch up on all the gossip while me and George go fishing . . . I wonder how often Rosemary will let him come, she can be a bit of a drag you know.'

'There aren't many women who put up with what I do' Mavis said angrily and she made her way to the buffet car.

* * *

'You'll never get watches like this again, this is an offer of a lifetime. Now all I'm asking is ten pounds a piece, they retail at at least fifty pounds, now whose going to take these last few off my hands?'

'Alright, I'll have one Guv'nor' the little man in the cap at the back of the crowd shouted.

'No you won't Sir, and neither will anyone else! Now clear away please, you're blocking the way in!'

The man in the uniform shunted away the small crowd.

'I don't know what you think you're doing mate, but this isn't a market, it's a motorway cafe, now pack up that suitcase and off you go.'

'Give a chap a chance, I've only been here a few minutes. Look you can have one of these watches if you turn a blind eye,'

'It's more than my jobs worth' said the security man. 'Now I won't tell you again.'

Dave grudgingly packed his case and headed back to his car.

'Miserable old devil' he thought, 'Still maybe I'll be lucky down at the harbour. Might be able to shift a bit of gear, shame it's not the holiday season, still there's always the locals.'

Dave was visiting George and Rosemary alone, as his second wife had left him on account of his 'shady deals.' He'd never been the most secure of men.

Although, two women had bravely taken the plunge and married him, only to come out drowning. He'd always had big ideas that never came to anything, but having said that, he'd been a good friend to Rosemary and George in his own way, and he hadn't had a holiday for a while, being 'a bit short of the readies' as Dave put it, so they thought a break would do him good.

✳ ✳ ✳

The red Jaguar sped along the country lanes.

'I'm glad we decided to come this way on the scenic route, not that this car couldn't whack 'em into fits on the motorway. Fast lane all the way, 0 to 60 mph in 10 seconds the dealer said, mind you, you only get what you pay for.'

'Fast lane all the way eh? Not with me in it you wouldn't and anyway, I rather liked the old car, it had a better inside mirror' said Sylvia, as she applied a fresh coat of lipstick rather shakily as William took another bend too quickly.

'In my position, one needs a prestige car, must keep up appearances.'

'None of them will have a car as classy as this one William.'

'No, you are right there Mother' William agreed, as he turned slightly and nodded to the passenger in the back seat of the car.

'Of course, none of them had the 'go' in them to succeed like you did.'

'Yes, you're right you know Mother, it takes more than sitting in an office to run one's own engineering firm. Of course they don't realise this, they just think I've had a bit of luck.'

'Well I think Rosemary and George have done well.' Sylvia butted in.

'Yes, but it's only a small place, anyone can run a hotel' Martha said.

'I'd like to see you try' Sylvia replied.

'Now come on you two, stop arguing, we'll be stopping shortly.'

Sylvia was right in her statement though. Martha was the last person on earth that would be capable of doing such a thing. Her late husband Arthur had always had money and she'd had an easy life. She'd had a daily help, a gardener, even a nanny when William was born.

He had gone away to boarding school, so she'd only seen him in the holidays. Her late husband Arthur and herself had given him every encouragement and an ample supply of money to start his business.

Now he was in his early forties, slightly receding, and with a bit of a pot belly, although still quite handsome.

Sylvia was about thirty-five, always had her short blond hair looking immaculate and her make up was so perfect, one would often wonder if her good looks were natural or due to a careful artistic application of lipstick and eye make-up.

Williams' mother, Martha, was about seventy. A slightly built lady with sharp violet eyes to match the rinse on her hair. She wore those half lens glasses and used to peer over them rather disapprovingly.

'Shall we stop at this cafe?' Sylvia asked 'I could do with touching up my hair.'

'I don't like the look of this place,' said William speeding past, 'We'll stop at a nice little cottage and have a Devon Cream tea.'

* * *

The girl in the red sweater gazed longingly at Peter. 'I'll miss you,' she sighed.

'I'll miss you too petal, but it won't be for long and I've promised Celia a break.'

'Why promise her anything? What about me?'

'Must keep her sweet you know, you wouldn't want her to stop my nights out would you?'

'Goodness no Peter, I don't see enough of you as it is.'

'Well, lets have one more drink then, before I go. Gin and tonic for you is it?'

'You're not trying to get me tipsy are you?' she giggled.

Peter waited by the bar as Sally totted off to the the Ladies. He looked at her in her tight skirt, which showed all her curves.

'Nice little figure,' he thought, 'But getting a bit too serious, glad I'm having this break. It will keep Celia sweet. I don't want her suspecting anything, and I fancy a bit of a change myself.'

When he arrived home, Celia had his dinner in the oven, and the cases packed.

'Shame you had to work late again,' she said. 'Still everything is done, we'll go to bed after dinner, so you'll be fresh for tomorrow's journey.'

'Yes my love,' he replied as he looked over at Celia, bending over the oven, 'I wish she'd lose a bit of weight and do herself up a bit. She wouldn't be too bad if she did.' he thought.

'Sylvia always kept herself nice. William's a lucky blighter,' he mused as he tucked into his steak and kidney pie. He imagined her on the beach in her bikini, with her blonde hair shining in the sun.

'Very nice' he sighed.

'What is?' Celia asked.

'Er . . . the steak and kidney pie my love, it's absolutely delicious.'

✳ ✳ ✳

'Fancy a stroll round to the station Rosemary?'

'Oh goodness, is that the time?' Rosemary replied. 'Yes, we had better get a move on George. But we can't walk there, what about Simons' fishing gear, he won't just be bringing his suitcase will he?'

'I never thought, I'll get the car.' George went out whistling to himself.

'I think he's quite looking forward to seeing Simon,'Rosemary thought to herself. 'He hasn't made many friends since we've been here.'

When they arrived, the train was already in the station.

Rosemary felt a bit disappointed. She wasn't keen on diesel trains, she loved the old steam engines, but she always liked to see them pull in at the station.

George spotted Simon and Mavis first.

'Look, there he is, just carrying his precious rods.'

'Never changes does he?' laughed Rosemary. And then she spotted Mavis, laden down like an old mule.

'Quick George, lets give Mavis a hand.'

'How are you, you old rascal?' George patted Simon

on the back and went to get the cases of Mavis.

'Had a good journey?' Rosemary asked.

'Yes lovely scenery,' Mavis replied.

'Oh Mavis, I've missed you, it's great to see you. Come on, let's get you to the hotel, you look like you could do with nice cup of tea!'

'Let's have a look at this bar of yours then George, Rosemary's told Mavis all about it in her letters. We'll have a few drinks and discuss our fishing trip.'

When they arrived at the hotel, Rosemary went upstairs with Mavis to help her unpack.

'It's a lovely place you've got here Rosemary.'

'Yes it is rather, isn't it? I feel it's a rather cosy sort of place, a home from home. I feel it's more like a large guest house than a hotel.'

'I know what you mean, hotels seem very formal.' Mavis said as she opened the window. 'Oh what a lovely view from this room Rosemary.'

'I know, Torquay is so hilly and if you happen to be at the top of a hill, you've got some really good sea views.'

'You're looking well you know Rosemary, this sea air must be doing you good.'

'Yes, it is, but the whole place is doing me good. I've always loved it down here, even as a child you know.'

'God we've know each other years haven't we Mavis, we've had some good times.'

'We sure have,' Mavis sighed longingly. 'What about the sixties? All those great discos, the 'flower power'; we did have some fun didn't we Rosemary?'

She sounded as if she was trying to convince herself.

'I'll say we did.' agreed Rosemary.

'You know I'll be forty next year,' said Mavis.

'Lucky, you wait till your past forty like me, and you know what they say.'

'I don't believe it about life begins at forty. I feel it's a sort of critical stage in life, you know. What have I done, where am I going?

If I've only got twenty years left, what am I going to do until then?'

'So you're going to die at sixty are your Mavis? You could live 'till you're ninty!'

'And I could die tomorrow Rosemary.'

She turned away and carried on with the unpacking. .

So Rosemary made her way down to the kitchen to see Lil.

'So I want that special menu for eight o'clock tonight as arranged.'

'I've got the normal meals to make as well Ma'am,' said Lil as she wiped the hair out of her eyes as she was cutting the kidney beans. She looked rather red in the face. 'And Mary's gone out without doing the potatoes.'

'But didn't you send her to get some prawns down by the harbour?'

'Yes . . . I know that, but if you hadn't insisted on prawn cocktails I'd have had her here where I can keep an eye on her. She's probably looking in all the shops or gazing out to sea instead of working with me like she's supposed to.'

Lil slammed down the collander full of beans.

'Now look here,' Rosemary turned sharply, 'I hardly ever interfere with you. I know you regard this kitchen as your domain. Normally we have straight forward English cooking for the guests but this is the first time that my friends have seen the hotel. They've travelled a long way, and I want their first meal here to be special.'

'Hmm, I suppose you're right.' Lil agreed reluctantly. 'I can see you wanting to make a good impression, it's just that I wish Mary would hurry up.'

'Look, I'll do the prawn cocktails when she gets here' said Rosemary. 'You concentrate on doing your famous orange sauce for the ducks Lil, and Mary can set the tables and finish the cleaning. The others should be here about tea time. We'll have dinner around eight.

Now where's George, I wanted him to put some flowers in the rooms, if I can drag him away from Simon for five minutes!'

Simon and George were sitting in the corner of the bar with two large brandy's as Rosemary walked in.

'Come and join us,' Simon said 'What about a nice sweet sherry?'

'No thanks, not at the moment, I've got an awful lot to do before the others arrive, but what about taking one up to Mavis while she's unpacking?'

'Never drinks in the daytime, does Mavis.' replied Simon.

'I was wondering George, if you could get some more green beans out of the garden and pick a few roses. I want the rooms to look nice.'

'Don't get putting any in my room, hay fever, you know' said Simon.

'At this time of the year?' Rosemary said.

'Yes they make me sneeze!'

＊ ＊ ＊

Simon sat on the garden bench as George cut the roses.

'So you like it here then George?'

'Best move we ever made. I didn't think so to start with, Rosemary was keener than me. She loves going for long walks along the beach, though I'm beginning to really like the place myself now.'

'Well I can't wait to get a boat out up the River Dart and do some fishing. I wonder if William has brought his rods?'

'He'll probably have the best money can buy' replied George.

'Good rods don't make the fisherman, it's skills' said Simon as they strolled into the house.

By six o'clock they had all arrived except Dave. Sylvia had gone up to her room to get ready. William was in the bar with George, Simon and Peter talking about his business and how well he was doing, with the odd inquiry about the hotel. Peter was asking about the local talent.

The women were in the garden.

'I must take you to see Torre Abbey one day' Rosemary said excitedly. 'There's the Agatha Christie room, rather like a shrine.'

'You've always been a great Agatha Christie fan haven't you?' said Celia.

'I know' said Rosemary 'I love a good who dunnit.'

'I rather like romantic novels myself' Celia sighed.

'Yes but they're all a load of rubbish' Mavis chipped in.

'I know' agreed Rosemary, 'I don't know any man in real life that would say all those romantic things, George doesn't anyway, he's so practical. When I'm upset, instead of a loving arm around me or a gentle kiss, he just says 'Come along Rosemary, pull yourself together, no good getting in a state.'

'Peter's quite understanding really' said Celia.

'Aren't you lucky' said Mavis. 'Simon understands his bloody fish more than he does me.'

Rosemary laughed. 'Come along girls, after this lovely meal that I've arranged for us it might even mellow our men! Miracles can happen sometimes you know.'

✳ ✳ ✳

Nice drop of claret this George' said Simon.

'And if I may add' Peter sighed contentedly, 'A lovely meal Rosemary, haven't had such a tasty duck in years.'

'I know, it is rather good isn't it. I can't take credit

18

for it, it's all down to our cook, Lil.'

'I always find duck a little too fatty for me' said Sylvia 'must keep an eye on the calories you know.'

'You don't need to watch your figure' Peter smiled.

Martha gave him a stern glance. 'I hope they don't start flirting in front of William' she thought, 'he deserves someone better.'

'So you're thinking of expanding are your William?' George changed the subject.

'Well I'd like to, need a few more funds. Must take the Bank manager to lunch.'

'I'd have thought money was the least of your problems' smirked Rosemary.

'That's what everyone thinks' said William. 'I'd like to get a bit of overseas trade, get into the European market.'

'Worse thing we could have done, joining the EEC' said Simon, 'should have stayed by ourselves.'

'British through and through, that's our Simon' laughed George.

'If you ever need any help, I'm pretty good at selling and I know a fair bit about the engineering trade' said Peter.

'Thanks old chap, I'll keep it mind. I say, where's Dave got to?'

'God knows' said Rosemary. 'He should have been here hours ago, I can't think what's happened to him.'

'Shame he's missed such a marvellous meal. Wasn't it delicious Mother?' said William as he helped Martha out of her chair.

'Surely the guests don't get this sort of food, duck and prawns?'

'Don't be ridiculous' Rosemary snapped. 'We do plain good English cooking, I couldn't possibly afford this. It was just a special meal to welcome you all!'

'I'm glad to hear it' Martha replied.

'Come along mother, let's go and join the others.' William took her by the arm and quickly escorted her out looking rather embarrassed.

Rosemary and George were in the kitchen filling up the dishwasher as they had let the staff leave early.

'Damn cheek' said George, 'What business is it of hers anyway. I've a good mind . . . '

'Oh forget it George, you know what Martha's like.'

'I can't for the life of me think why you invited her' said George. 'I'm sure William would have liked to have got away from her for a while.'

'You know he's tied to her apron strings' said Rosemary angrily.

'And her purse string.' a voice said.

They both turned round as Sylvia came into the kitchen.

'Oh look I'm sorry Sylvia, we didn't mean to say . . .' George stammered.

'I did' Sylvia said. 'Don't apologise, he's frightened to say or do anything in case she stops his allowance. It makes me sick.' She walked to the sink and started to sponge a food stain off her dress.

When she had finished she came over and sat at the large pine table in the kitchen.

'Look don't be embarrassed, in front of me. Nothing I hear about my 'dear mother-in-law' surprises me. There's no love lost between us as you both know. Anyway enough of this talk,' She took George by the arm 'Come on if you treat me to a large brandy I promise your secret will be safe with me.'

Rosemary laughed as she finished putting the plates away.

The rest of the evening passed by quite pleasantly. Chatting and talking about old times, and Rosemary and George suggesting ideas and various places to visit.

Around midnight they all retired.

CHAPTER THREE

The fly in the ointment

Simon was standing over the dining table holding a giant fish. 'Are we having this for tea!' The blood was dripping all over the table.

'Fish for tea! Rosemary, fish for tea! Rosemary, Rosemary.'

'Take it away, take it away!'

She jumped up suddenly in a sweat and looked at the alarm. It was three o'clock in the morning.

'What a funny dream' she thought.

'Rosemary! Rosemary! George!'

'Am I still dreaming?' she thought. Then she heard a banging at the door. She shook George.

'Oh what's going on? Go back to sleep Rosemary' George muttered.

'There's someone downstairs George.'

'Who?' said George.

'How the hell do I know? Will you get up and see?'

George stumbled out of bed and fell over Rosemary's

electric rollers.

'Oh my bloody foot!' he groaned.

'For God's sake George you'll wake the others up. Just get a move on!'

George finally hobbled to the front door, his toe throbbing.

'Oh it's you. What happened?'

'Damn car broke down' Dave said despondantly.

'Aren't you in the AA?' asked George.

'Don't need 'em. I can usually fix it myself. It's just about got me down here, but I don't think I'll be able to drive it anymore. Can I put it in one your garages George?'

'Sorry, they're all taken. William put his in the last one tonight, and there's no room on the drive. Leave it in the road. Anyway, nobody is going to pinch that wreck.'

'No, but I've got a bit of stock in the back.' Dave said hesitantly.

'He never changes' thought George. 'Well leave it there for now and maybe we can put it somewhere tomorrow. Though I don't think Rosemary will be too pleased.'

'Now for God sake, show Dave to his bedroom before he wakes the whole house up.' Rosemary had come down the stairs.

'Hello old gal' said Dave, and planted a kiss on her cheek, nearly knocking her over.

'Not so much of the old!' laughed Rosemary, and

ambled back upstairs.

'Come on Dave,' said George grabbing his suitcase, 'You look a bit dirty, do you want a quick shower before you retire? Don't make too much noise though!'

'I'm starving. Haven't had anything for hours.'

'Hang on, I'll see what I can rustle up.'

George came back after a couple of minutes with a can of lager from the bar and a cheese sandwich.

'This will have to do for now Dave.'

'Thanks mate' said Dave. 'It'll tide me over until breakfast.'

'Thank God for that!' George said as he went back upstairs to bed.

⁂ ⁂ ⁂

Next morning they breakfasted at the same time as the few guests at Rosemary's request, as she didn't want to annoy Lil anymore than necessary.

After tucking into bacon and eggs, they sat on the terrace to drink their coffee, deciding what they would all do for the day.

As expected, George and Simon had got a day's fishing planned. William rather unexpectedly decided against joining them, although Simon did manage to persuade him to lend him one of his expensive rods.

'Now watch what you're doing with it' William said, as he handed it over.

'I shall treat it like a new born baby' Simon replied,

caressing the rod in his hands.

Mavis told William to stop worrying as Simon considered all fishing tackle so precious he would do just that.

Martha kept saying she would like to go shopping but did not feel like going alone, so Celia volunteered to go with her.

'So kind of you dear, at my age one finds it rather tiring with all these hills.'

Rosemary suggested to the rest of them that they visit Cockington, a lovely old village that was only a short distance away.

A long steep winding lane with high hedgerows led to Cockington. These were dense and although it was shaded from the sun, it looked very green and restful and was pleasant to walk down.

When they reached the village, it was far prettier than any picture postcard with thatched cottages covered in masses of pink and white roses, and an old Blacksmith's that was now a gift shop with hundreds of brasses hanging outside that glistened in the sunlight. In the square were horse and carriages that were taking people to and from the village along another lane that led to the sea. It looked just like they had stepped back in time.

Rosemary gave them a guided tour all around the lakes and the country park.

'Don't you just love it here' she sighed. 'You should see it in Spring, the woods are full of primroses, like a yellow carpet beneath your feet.'

'I must admit it's so unspoilt, so peaceful' agreed Mavis.

'Down on the green, the Manor House is busy in summer, they have fêtes and things going on, and there is a little church that's centuries old.'

'Shall we go and see it?' Mavis asked

'I don't like these old churches, they're musty and depressing' Dave groaned.

'How do you know you haven't been in one for years have you?'

'Well my feet are killing me. Can't we go and have some tea?' Sylvia bent down and started rubbing her toes.

'I'll go with with Mavis' William offered.

'We'll see you later in the Old Mill Cafe then.' Rosemary said, and the rest of them made their way back down the hill with Sylvia hobbling behind them on high heel stilettos.

✳ ✳ ✳

As they entered the church, William grabbed Mavis's arm.

'Why haven't you answered any of my letters?'

'Oh William, what's the point, nothing can come of it.'

'Look Mavis, people can't change their feelings. How you put up with him is beyond me. I'd never leave you alone like he does.'

She walked ahead of him down the aisle of the old church. She'd walked this way twenty years ago, twenty wasted years.

'Why me?' She thought.' 'I'm so plain not a bit like Sylvia. In a way I ought to be grateful that William cares for me, I'd probably get no one else at my age.'

Yet she didn't do herself justice. Mavis had lovely green eyes and her mousey hair was tied in a pony tail, with the right grooming she could have looked quite attractive.

She walked to the altar and nervously picked up a hymn book, and started flicking though the pages.

'I loved that dress Sylvia had on last night at dinner. She looked gorgeous.' She said stammering.

'And you could look just as good Mavis.'

'I don't know why you bother with me William.'

'Look, Sylvia may look good, but she's never give a damn about me. You're a kind and caring person. You think about others, that's something Sylvia could never do.'

He pulled her towards him and gazed at her longingly. He brushed her cheek with his hand and brought his lips closer to hers. She could stand the temptation no longer, but she had to she thought.

She didn't know how she found the will power, but she pushed him away and ran back up the aisle.

'Mavis, stop!' William pleaded.

She turned at the door of the little church.

'We must go William the others will be be wondering where we are.'

* * *

It was mid afternnon. They had all gone out except Sylvia who was soaking in the bath, when she heard someone opening the door. It was Peter. She grabbed a towel angrily.

'Don't you believe in knocking? What are you doing here anyway?'

What's the matter with you Sylvia? There is no one here. Anyway fancy grabbing that towel. It isn't as if I haven't seen it all before.'

'Yes, but you're not going to again!' She quickly went into the bedroom and put her silk robe on.

'Come on you know you want me really.' he pushed her down on the bed.

'You don't need me, you've got plenty of women.'

'Well actually I've been behaving myself lately. Anyway you're different, you and me are meant to be together. Can you honestly look me in the eyes and say you don't fancy me anymore.'

'Even if I do fancy you, it doesn't mean I'm going to give in again.' Sylvia tossed her head back indignantly.

'You will! You'll get bored down here, when the novelty of sight-seeing wears off. You know I'm the only exciting thing here.' He grabbed her roughly and kissed her, and went out of the room laughing.

She angrily started to do her hair and knocked an unsealed bottle of nail varnish on the bedroom floor.

'Oh damn!' she said angrily mopping it up. 'You know he's right' she thought to herself. 'What with William wrapped up with his mother and the business and Martha keeping an eye on her, so she didn't upset her precious son! Maybe Peter was right, she'd go mad. He was the only bit of excitement here.'

She tied her silk robe and made her way to Peter's room.

Mary was just going to the airing cupboard with the linen, when she caught sight of Sylvia going into Peter's room.

'What's going on?' she thought to herself. 'I thought things like this only happened in the big hotels in town, that Mother warned me about.'

CHAPTER FOUR

The casino

The evening meal was filled with talk of George's and Simon's fishing.

'I think we'll take a boat out from the harbour tomorrow, if you like Simon.' George suggested.

'Sounds good to me.' Simon sounded like an excited child.

'Don't mind do you Mavis?' George asked hesitantly.

'Of course she doesn't mind, got loads to do haven't you dear?' Simon added.

Rosemary was getting fed up with the fishing talk and so was everyone else by the looks of things. Rosemary suggested a night out at the casino in town. Dave piped up immediately.

'Rather, I fancy my chances at the roulette wheel.'

'You rely on chance too much Dave!' William said 'That's not the way to get money, it's just damned hard work that gets you anywhere in this life.'

'A bit of luck as well though, surely?' Rosemary said.

'Yes and also it's who you know not what you know. I've found that out' Simon said.

'Gambling! You might just as well throw your money down the drain.' Martha butted in.

Sylvia stood up 'Well I think it's a great idea, we could all do with a night out, don't you agree girls?' Mavis and Celia nodded.

'That's settled then I'm going to get changed, though I haven't the faintest idea what to wear.' she muttered as she left the room.'

Mavis put on the one and only decent dress she possessed, cream silk with a low neck and long sleeves and a fish tail bottom. She stood in front of the full length mirror. 'Not bad' she thought to herself. She'd always had a neat little figure but when she looked at her face, it seemed rather chubby.

When she knew all the men were downstairs in the bar, she knocked on Sylvia's door.

'Hello darling! You look nice. What a lovely dress.' Sylvia said as she struggled to put the back on her diamente earing.

'Let me,' said Mavis.

'Oh thanks. You are a love. These damn things.'

'I was wondering Sylvia, if you could do my make-up for me?'

'Of course' Sylvia got out a huge box with every conceivable colour of eye shadows and lipsticks you could imagine. Mavis looked a little nervous.

'Now don't worry, I'll only do it subtle. Now I think

perhaps soft beige and a peach lipstick to go with that cream dress.'

Sylvia might not have been good at many things, but she certainly knew the art of make-up and she set to work with various brushes.

When Sylvia had finished, Mavis came out of her room and bumped into Peter coming from the opposite end of the landing.

'I thought you were downstairs with the others,' Mavis said.

'Oh yes, I 'er just forgot my wallet. By the way Mavis, you look a bit of alright tonight.'

'Do you really think so Peter? she flushed.

'I certainly do! May I escort you downstairs my dear?' he laughed as she took his arm.

'My word, what's happened to our little mouse' Rosemary thought to herself as Peter and Mavis came into the room. She looks lovely!'

Simon looked up in amazement.

'Well old chap, your wife certainly looks the business tonight. ' George said.

'Bloody waste of money that dress was. I told her. Mind you, it doesn't look too bad.'

William stood by the fireplace and said nothing, but his mind was full. 'My darling you do look wonderful' he thought, 'but you could come down in a sack and you'd still look good to me.'

❋ ❋ ❋

As George was a member of the Casino he signed them all in. It was very luxurious, with deep red pile carpets and the most magnificent chandeliers.

'My word this place is the business, I could get used to coming here.' Dave said as he looked around in admiration.

'Yes, get used to it for five minutes for that's how long it'll take you to lose your money' William said smugly.

'Well I feel lucky tonight, you never know I could make my fortune'Dave replied confidently.

'How do you think they pay for this décor – from people like you that fritter their money away.' Martha interrupted the men's conversation.

'I'm sure they can do without Dave's ten pounds, they're looking for business men with money' George remarked.

As they all went into the lounge George took Rosemary to one side 'Try and keep Martha in here with you girls, she'll only spoil it for us.'

'Okay, but we want to come into the gambling rooms later and have a little flutter. I don't want to be stuck with her all night.'

The casino was quite busy that evening, although the men managed to get some seats at one of the tables where the minimum bet was fifty pence.

Surprisingly Dave did win about forty pounds, but instead of cashing in his chips, as they all advised him to, he carried on playing and lost it all.

'I told you didn't I!' William said rather pleased with

himself.

'Oh well you only live once. At least I've enjoyed myself. You haven't even had a bet.'

'That's because I like to watch and make a note of the numbers.'

'You're just a mean old sod, no wonder you've got so much money. You can't take it with you you know.'

'How dare you! I've worked hard for all my money!!' William sounded quite aggressive.

'Now come on you two' Simon tried to calm them down, which was quite out of character 'We'll go back into the bar, it's bloody ridiculous not to be able to get a drink in here. You can treat me Dave with your winnings.

'Sorry old chap, but I blew it all. I'm afraid the drinks will have to be on you'

'Come on then' Simon said grudgingly. 'By the way, where's Peter got to?'

They started to look around the place and finally found him hidden in a corner, talking to a most attractive brunette, wearing a rather short dress. She looked quite affluent, judging by the jewellery she was wearing.

Simon barged in 'You don't want to bother with him love, he's got no money. Coming for a drink with us Peter?

The lady in question smiled rather seductively 'I'd better let you run along with your friends' She turned and walked away.

Peter was furious. 'I was in there. She was a bit of alright. Did you see her legs? I've never seen legs like them. You've ruined my chances!!'

Simon put his arm round Peters shoulder

'Now don't be like that, you couldn't have got off with her, not with the girls in the lounge, be sensible.'

'Well I could have arranged to see her again.'

'You wouldn't have had the money to take her to the places she'd be used to.' Dave added.

'Oh I suppose you're right, come on then lads I'll buy you a drink.'

'That's more like it . . . I knew you'd see sense.' Simon smiled.

＊ ＊ ＊

Tom was digging away at the vegetable patch. 'Good morning ladies. Lovely day.'

'Good morning' Mavis and Sylvia replied.

'You're both up early, mind you, a stroll before breakfast does give you a good appetite, doesn't it?'

'Well I didn't sleep very well' said Mavis 'And I can't just lie there in bed.'

'And I was up early doing my exercises' said Sylvia 'I think this sea air is so good for the complexion, provided you wear moisturiser, that is!'

'I must say,' said Mavis 'You look very fit for your age.'

'Do you think so!' said Sylvia flushing with pleasure.

'Well actually, I meant Tom, but you look good too!' Mavis added rather embarassed.

'Anyway, I'm going for a quick jog before breakfast' Sylvia said and off she went.

'What's your secret then Tom?' Mavis laughed 'Pills and potions?'

'Well you expect to get a few aches and pains at my age' he said 'But really, it's just a happy and contented life, counts for a lot you know young lady.' and he carried on with his digging.

Mavis blushed. 'Fancy thinking I'm young, when I'm heading for the 'big 40' next birthday' She thought to herself day dreaming.

She was suddenly bought back to earth by the sound of Peter's voice.

'I'll help you later Tom,' Peter strolled down the garden path.

'That's very kind of you.'

'Nonsense I'd enjoy it, Our garden at home isn't very big.'

'Well you could always get an allotment if you're that keen on growing vegetables.'

'Mmm, I might consider doing that Tom.'

'Well I'm going in now' said Mavis. 'Are you coming for breakfast Peter?'

'Yes I'll be in shortly.' he answered.

'By the way sir, I've managed to find you that book on roses.'

'Thanks Tom and less of the sir, I'm no gentleman'

he laughed.

'It's in the shed, I'll go and get it for you.'

'Don't worry, I'll get it, you've enough to do.'

He got the book and joined the others for breakfast.

CHAPTER FIVE

Dartmoor

The following day at Rosemary's suggestion they decided to have a day out at Dartmoor. Although Sylvia tried to put them all off, saying how windy and desolate it would be. Rosemary convinced then how beautiful it was with all the coloured heathers and the ponies running wild and its enchanting remoteness.

They were getting ready to leave and Martha was sitting on the terrace reading. Peter came out and she turned her head to look at him, peering over her glasses. He walked to the end of the terrace and looked out towards the sea.

'Looks like it'll be a nice day on the moors.'

'You can never rely on the English weather, it looks cloudy to me.' Martha moaned.

'Now don't be a killjoy, they're all putting their comfortable shoes and trainers on!' he laughed.

'Anyway, I'd like a word with you while we're alone for a moment.' Martha closed her book. 'Don't think I don't know what's going on between you and Sylvia!'

'I don't know what you're talking about,' Peter put his hands in his pockets and started whistling.

'Quite frankly, if I didn't think it would interfere with William's business I'd give you my blessing. she's always bled him dry. Good riddance I'd say! But at the moment William couldn't have the publicity of a divorce, it would be bad for his business.'

She stood up and slammed down her book

'So I'm telling you to keep away from Sylvia.'

'And if I don't?' asked Peter.

'If you don't, I'll tell Celia!'

'She'll never believe you.'

'Won't she? You've hidden a lot of your other affairs from her, but she's not as stupid as you think. If she was offered proof.'

Just then the others came out and Peter walked away.

✳ ✳ ✳

The two cars made their way along the narrow country lanes through the village of Ashburton and out to the moors. George in his old Rover could barely keep up with William and nearly lost him at one point, till somebody saw a flash of him in the distance.

'He's going a bit too fast down these lanes' George thought 'If ever he meets a car coming the other way, there's barely room for two to pass.'

They reached Dartmoor to be greeted by masses of purple heather and yellow gorse. It was a beautiful sight and although it had been warm in Torquay, it was quite windy on the moors.

They had walked a short distance across Dartmoor when Sylvia said 'I've trodden in a cow pat or something and she sat down and wiped the mess of her black high heeled patent shoes.

'What a ridiculous pair of shoes to wear for walking on the Moors!'

William turned and looked at her in disgust.

'Well I didn't know we'd be doing all this walking. I thought we'd just go into the village at Widecomb on the Moor.'

'You can't come all this way and not explore.' said George.

'You know Rosemary, I think you've got a spare pair of trainers in the boot. I'll go and get them for Sylvia.'

'I'm not wearing those things, I'd rather stay where I am.'

'Well I'm rather tired,' said Martha I'll just sit for a bit while you lot go off. Perhaps I could get the hampers ready.'

'Well I think I'll try those trainers then George, if you wouldn't mind getting them for me.' Sylvia said rather quickly as she dreaded the thought of having to stay with Martha.

When they were all ready to go, Celia decided at the last minute, 'I think I'll stay here, I feel rather tired.'

Peter felt a wave of panic come over him. 'Don't be silly darling, the air will do you good, it might even wake you up if you feel tired' he said nervously.

'No I think I'll rest, you lot go ahead.'

Peter couldn't persuade Celia no matter how hard he tried.

'Come on Peter' Dave dragged him away by the arm. 'You don't want to stop with Martha surely? Anyway I've got some business I want to discuss with you' and Peter was lead away reluctantly.

'Don't you think this place is romantic?' Rosemary asked Mavis and Sylvia.

'I know, you can almost see Kathy and Heathcliff running over the Moors.' Sylvia said.

'Well they did film Wuthering Heights here.' Rosemary informed them. They reached one peak and sat at the top while the men were down below. It was quite windy and Mavis was holding her ear.

'Are you alright?' Rosemary inquired.

'Just a bit of earache. I should have worn a hat or scarf really.'

'Let's not stay up here then let's get back, I might have one in the car.' Rosemary shouted down to the others 'Shall we make tracks back now? Lunch will probably be ready.'

Celia seemed quite relaxed and normal when Peter came back much to his relief.

'Well I don't think Martha has said anything to her yet' he thought, 'perhaps she's giving me a chance to finish with Sylvia.'

The fresh air had given them all an appetite, and they tucked into the hampers like greedy children.

✷ ✷ ✷

Martha stood on the terrace doing her deep breathing exercises.

'What's all this then?' George laughed. 'Are you in training Martha?'

'I'm hoping this sea air will loosen my catarrh. I suffer dreadfully from it you know. I normally have to take tablets to clear it.'

'Yes thinking about it, Rosemary's had fewer colds since we've been here.'

'And are you making it pay George?' Martha changed the subject.

'We're ticking over nicely. No big profits yet. I think we're just breaking even when we've paid the bills and the staff.'

'Perhaps you need to advertise more and do a few bargain breaks for the pensioners.'

'Mmm that sounds like a good idea. I'll mention it to Rosemary.'

Just at that moment William came out. 'Oh there you are Mother, I was wondering if you'd like to come for a walk?'

'You, walk! You normally drive everywhere.' She looked over at him. He looked rather green. 'Are you feeling alright dear? You look ill. I hope it's nothing you've eaten.'

'Not here it's not' George said defensively 'damn good stuff Lil serves up.'

'It's more like too much to drink' William said feebly.

'Yes you have been knocking it back a bit lately, old chap!' George said.

'It's that damn woman, she's driving you to drink.'

'What woman Mother?' he muttered nervously.

'Sylvia, of course' Martha replied. 'Come with me William, I've got a bottle of Milk of Magnesia upstairs. A dose of that will put you right.'

She went out with William trailing behind, just as Rosemary came out onto the terrace.

'What was all that about?' she asked.

'Oh just Martha doing her domineering mother bit!' replied George as Rosemary began to straighten the umbrellas on the tables. 'Martha suggested that we advertise a few bargain breaks for pensioners. It seems like a good idea, don't you think?'

'Mmm, I suppose.' said Rosemary.

'She has an eye for business. She's helped William a lot' George added.

'Well she had the money to do it.'

'Yes, but she seems to know what she's talking about. Let's sit and have a coffee and talk about it while it's quiet.'

'Not now' Rosemary snapped, 'I've got a lot to do.' And she went out.

'Seems a bit touchy lately' thought George, 'It must be her hormones playing up again.'

CHAPTER SIX

A life on the ocean wave

The cars came to a crossroads that said 'Upper or Lower Ferry'.

'The Kingswear ferry always has a long wait we'll take this one,' Rosemary said poking George in the back of the neck.

'God I love Dartmouth' sighed Simon 'I think I was born before my time. I should have been a fisherman in the last century, casting the nets out, selling your catch at the end of the day.'

'Yes and the fish tasted a lot better then, than they do now with all the rubbish that's dumped in our seas and rivers.' George said reminisingly.

'Are the others still behind?' Mavis enquired.

'Yes I can see them out of my mirror I should think we'll all board the ferry together.'

As they slowed down to the approach of the ferry crossing there was only a small queue of cars ahead and they boarded the first one.

As the ferry crossed the River Dart, Dartmouth looked splendid, with all the little cottages set high in the hills and the boats along the river.

After parking the cars with some difficulty when they reached the other side and Simon, moaning about the cost, even though it wasn't his car and George was paying. They all met up and strolled along the river's edge, which was quite charming, all the front had been paved in recent years, and black traditional style lamp posts were set all along. They found a small pub, down one of the quaint little side streets, and over drinks they discussed going on a boat trip.

'How long shall we have one or two hours?' Rosemary asked the others.

'Is it windy on deck?' enquired Sylvia.

'Well you can always go below.'

'I think an hour's plenty.' Simon intervened.

'Well Rosemary will get us a good deal She knows the owner of the one boat and there's a bar on board.'

'Is there really? Then lead the way George' Simon gulped down his drink.

As they approached the 'Queen of the Dart' a man with white hair and a beard who looked like a typical old Salt came up to Rosemary and gave her a hug. 'How are you my little treasure?' 'What's this works outing?' he joked.

'Oh just some friends staying with us.'

Rosemary made the introductions. 'This is Andy

everyone. George and I met him when we came down here one day and we feel like we've known him for years.'

'I suppose I'll have to do a good commentary for you. I'll wait for a few more passengers to board and then we'll be off'.

He went up to a small cabin on the poop deck in which he steered the boat. It had a microphone inside.

Simon went up to join him.

'How are you old mate. Simon's my name. I'm an old friend of George and Rosemary.' He shook his hand firmly. 'I'd love a job like yours. On the river. I love fishing. I suppose you fish a lot?'

'Well I do when I get the time, but I'm normally busy with the boat.'

'Even at this time of the year?'

'Well in the summer it's hectic, but even now we run plenty of trips for schools, and pensioners clubs who book the boat for the day.'

'Do you live local?'

'Yes. Actually there's my house.' he pointed to a small pink cottage set in the hill.

'Oh God!' You lucky blighter. I'd love that you know. A little fisherman's cottage by the river. I work in a factory. Wouldn't put a dog in there. Terrible place! I'll retire down here.'

'Do you think your wife would enjoy it?'

'Of course she would. She'd be mad if she didn't. By the way.' He stepped forward 'I've forgotten your name.'

'Andy'

'Oh yes of course, Andy. Can I bring you a pint up?'

'That's kind or you . . . er Simon. 'But I'm not allowed to drink while I'm operating the boat.'

'Oh just half then. I'll go and get you one' He wouldn't take no for an answer.

While Simon was in the bar Andy was furiously waving to George. George came up. 'Listen your friend Simon, nice chap and all that but can't have him up here while I'm operating the boat and doing the talk old man.'

'Oh yes he can be a bit of a nuisance, he's okay, salt of the earth though once you get to know him. Don't worry leave him to me.'

George met Simon at the bottom of the steps looking rather unsteady with the movement of the boat, holding a pint in one hand and a half in the other.

George took the half off him and Simon started to go back up the steps. 'Sorry Simon, no passengers allowed up there. Andy's rules I'm afraid.'

'But I was having a good chat with him.'

'Come on plenty to see down here we'll be off soon.'

The last few passengers boarded including a few noisy school children and they set off.

The boat went down the river towards the mouth of the sea and Andy gave the occasional commentary. He pointed out on the left a very exclusive Sailing club, that he had visited once as he was signed in by an affluent friend. Further down on the right was a little secluded cove surrounded by rocks. There was a very small house that a rich gentleman had built in the 18th century where his wife could change so she could bathe there as she was too shy to undress behind the trees.

'Did you hear that dear? What about building me something like that?' Sylvia nudged William.

'As if you would be too shy. You couldn't care less who saw you, even if you were naked.' Martha said in a hostile manner.

'Well at least I've got a good body. I don't mind who see's it.' She tossed her head back and walked away winking at Peter as she went passed.

'I don't suppose she does either' Rosemary giggled like a schoolgirl.

When it reached the mouth of the river close to the sea, the boat started to turn around and it became quite choppy.

Simon held on to the side and spilt his beer. He looked green.

Peter and George were in stitches. 'You, a sea fisherman! Stick to the river bank' George laughed.

Celia also felt sick so Mavis helped her to a seat.'

Andy spoke over the microphone to the passengers 'As soon as we've finished turning and go back up the river it will become calmer, ladies and gentlemen and would those children not get too near the sides. Thank you.'

A few minutes later they were heading back up the river.

It was a clear day and the view was lovely. The river glistened in the sun.

They passed the Royal Naval College and Agatha Christie's house, which was pointed out to all of them by Rosemary, long before Andy had spotted it. It was a magnificent white building set amongst the trees.

A little further along the river when they were out of Dartmouth and away from most of the boats and ferries the river widened. The banks were very green and it looked a tranquil setting.

Celia was feeling a lot better. She came on the top deck, sat in the sun and started to doze.

Simon meanwhile was boring everyone with talk of how he was leaving the Midlands to live in either Dartmouth or Brixham.

'I wish you had kept him up here with you Andy' George said as he poked his head inside the little cabin.

✳ ✳ ✳

Martha was on the lower deck. 'Shouldn't you be with your wife? I hear she wasn't feeling well' Martha lifted up the tinted clips on her glasses at an angle and peered at Peter disapprovingly.

'I think she's sleeping now. Anyway, she's a big girl, doesn't need me with her all the time.'

'When Arthur was alive, he was always there when I was feeling under the weather. He was a most considerate man.'

'Well he had the time to be. He was a man of leisure.'

'He still had to work to keep an eye on his investments.'

William was sitting nearby talking to Mavis. Martha called over to him 'I was just saying your father he never had it easy.'

'No well when you've got money it's hard work holding on to it. I've found that out. Still let's not talk of money.' He turned and smiled at Mavis.

George was standing at the stern with Sylvia. 'He's an handsome man, Andy, even though his hair is white, his tanned weather-beaten face gives him character. I think I rather like a more mature man.' Sylvia mused.

'So am I too young for you – late forties' George laughed.

'Any age will suffice as long as they have that certain something.'

'And I haven't?' asked George.

'You dear, sweet man, I know you're only teasing me. You and Rosemary are a perfect pair. Made for each other.'She studied his face.

George had a good head of hair for his age, mousey coloured but with a few streaks of grey. Many men of his age were starting to bald. He wasn't what you could call handsome, but he had pale green eyes that had a certain character to them.

'No he wasn't bad looking, old George, but too much of a steady type. Not for her' Sylvia thought to herself.

Mavis and Rosemary were sitting in the deck chairs

soaking up the sun.

'This weather's really warm for September.'

'Mm this is the life' Mavis sighed dreamily.

'You sound content.' said Rosemary. 'I was a little worried about you the day you arrived, You sounded so fed up with life and your age.'

'Oh I know I didn't mean to worry you. I was just feeling thoroughly cheesed off, you know how life gets at times.'

'I certainly do. I miss Sarah now she's at university. I mean she writes and comes down to visit but its not the same as having her here. And I worry about money. The bills at home were bad enough, but a hotel with the fuel, and final demands, and taxes. They say money doesn't buy happiness but it certainly helps.

'I know Simon keeps me short. I mean I know I'm earning but he moans when I ask for extra money towards the bills. Yet he always finds money for his nights out and fishing.'

'Still I do feel content now.' She lay back in the sun and closed her eyes. The boat glided gently along.

* * *

Simon had now decided to have a large brandy, and was thinking he might buy himself a blazer with a nautical crest on.

He left the bar and went outside on deck holding his glass.

There were some noisy boys running about. He pushed passed them. Suddenly he felt a little jolt. All he could hear were the children giggling. He went a bit peculiar. The next thing he knew he was in the water.

Suddenly a little old lady jumped up and screamed 'There's a man in the river.'

They all came running to find Simon splashing about in the water.

Andy tried to slow the boat down. 'Can he swim? I can't stop here. Are you alright?' He shouted to Simon' The schoolchildren were falling over themselves laughing. They had been getting bored with the trip. This was the highlight of their day.

'He looks just like a drunken duck splashing about in the water.' Rosemary said trying not to laugh.

George threw a lifebelt overboard and Andy made blasts on his horn, which meant man overboard. Just at that moment a man in a little fishing boat rowed up to Simon and pulled him on to his boat.

'I'll turn round and pick him up.' Andy shouted to the man in the boat.

'I suppose he was drunk as usual?' Mavis said as she watched him swaying unsteadily in the little fishing boat.

'I feel sorry for that poor man. Sitting there peacefully minding his own business. Simon will drive him mad. I bet the man wished he'd let him drown.'

'Oh you are awful' Rosemary said playfully.

Mavis looked sad. She turned to William 'I wish we

could have left him there.'

After a few minutes they all helped him on board, dripping wet and cold.

'You know how the fish feel now old chap' Peter laughed.

'I'm glad you all find it so funny' Simon could hardly speak.

They put a blanket around him and George took him into the bar and got him a drink.

'Do you think he should have anymore' Rosemary went to take the glass from George's hand.

'Well I should think he's sobered up by now and he feels really cold.'

'I lost my whisky flask in the water.' Simon said shivering. 'Scared the life out of me I can tell you. I could see my life flashing before me.'

'Well it's a good job you can swim.'

'Bloody good job that fisherman was there. Nice chap, we had a chat.'

'I'm sure you did.'

'How funny my life being saved by a fellow fisherman.'

'Well it will teach you not to drink so much.' Mavis prodded him with her finger.

'How dare you! I wasn't drunk.' He stood up and swayed a little.

'Of course you were drunk, Simon. Don't be ridiculous, you've been drinking ever since we boarded this boat.'

'Well, admittedly I've had a few but I wasn't drunk.'

So how come you fell overboard then?' Rosemary asked.

'I didn't fall over – I was pushed!! Simon said adamantly.

CHAPTER SEVEN

A tragedy

The following evening Lil was adding the final touches to the meal and stirring a large saucepan of boiling mussels. She turned to Mary. 'You can put the starters on the table when they're ready. It will give me a bit more room and I'll carve the lamb.'

Many quietly obeyed not wanting to upset her, as she had been in a mood all day.

Celia was sitting on the terrace reading a book when Rosemary came out.

'You're down early.'

'I know, i'm starving for some reason.'

'Well dinner won't be long, I'll just go and see how Lil's getting on.'

❋ ❋ ❋

William, George and Simon were in the bar having an evening drink before the meal.

Dave came rushing in.

'I say William, have you seen your car? Damn nasty scratch all over the wheel arch. Took all the paint off!'

Always the joker.' William laughed, 'Come and have a drink.'

He looked at Dave's face and realised he wasn't joking and they all went out to look at it.

'I can't believe someone would come on the drive and do this.' said Peter.

They were all kneeling down on the gravel inspecting it. William looked ashen.

'I didn't think you'd got vandals down here' he turned to George.

'You get them everywhere nowadays I suppose.' George remarked, 'Anyway, you're fully comp' aren't you? Don't worry, I know a good garage in town that will fix it for you.'

'Yes, but will they have the right shade of paint?'

What's going on?' Rosemary came out. 'Dinners ready you lot.'

The men knelt over the car like surgeons on an operating table all giving their opinions.

'Well there's nothing that can be done until tomorrow' said George standing up 'Let's go and have dinner.'

'I'm not a bit hungry' said William, as they went in. He looked despondent.

'Never mind son, don't let it upset your dinner, these mussels are delicious.'

It was a tasty meal of lamb followed by Lil's special apple pie.

Although the talk through most of the meal was William's car.

'Oh well' he thought 'as much as I love that car, it's only metal. When all said and done, if anything happened to Mavis that would be a real tragedy.' and he perked up.

They all retired to the lounge for coffee and brandy, but Celia said she was tired and went upstairs.

As the evening progressed, George, Rosemary, Peter and Mavis decided on a game of knockout whisk in partners. William, Dave and Sylvia were in the TV lounge, and Martha was on the terrace even though it was quite a chilly evening.

'Why didn't you trump over my hearts?' Rosemary said to George.

'Because I haven't got any trumps left!' he said angrily.

'Alright, there's no need to tell your opponents!'

'I haven't had a decent hand since this game began.'

Just then Martha staggered in holding her stomach. She gripped onto the back of the chair.

'Are you alright?' George asked.

'I've got dreadful stomach pains' she said, as she made her way slowly to the chair. 'It must have been those mussles.'

'Well everyone else is fine.' Rosemary said.

She looked over at Martha, although she was an old

moaner, she could see this time she didn't look well at all.

'Shall I get you a doctor?' she asked.

'No I'll be okay. I've got some of my own medicine. If you could just help me upstairs.'

Rosemary went to get William and they took her to her room.

'Are you sure you'll be alright Mother?'

'Yes William, don't fuss! A good nights sleep and I'll be fine tomorrow.'

Rosemary and William came back downstairs.

'I can't understand it' said Rosemary. 'We all had the same for dinner. Unless, she's caught a stomach bug or something.'

They finished their game of cards and after a few drinks, retired for the night.

The following morning, William was making such a noise in the shower he woke Sylvia. She peeped out of the sheets.

'You're up early, what time is it?'

It's only about seven thirty. I thought I'd go to see how mother is. She mightn't feel like coming down for breakfast, so I thought I'd ask Rosemary for some dry toast and weak tea to take up to settle her stomach.'

Sylvia curled back up underneath the quilt.

William knocked on Martha's door, but got no reply. So he went downstairs.

He heard noises coming from the kitchen.. Rosemary and Mary were running about preparing the breakfasts.

'Good morning, everything okay?'

'No it isn't' she snapped. 'Lil's not well she can't come in this morning. It's unlike her. She never lets us down. Mary did you and Lil have mussels last night?'

'Well, yes we did actually ma'am' Mary answered cautiously.

'Well it's funny Martha and Lil should be ill. Lil is so particular. She'd only have served those that were opened. She'd have thrown the unopened ones away. Anyway, will you excuse me William? I must get this bacon on.'

'Okay, I'll get out of your way. I'll pop back up and see if mother's awake yet.'

Just as he was mounting the stairs, he heard a scream. He ran up. Sylvia was standing at the door of Martha's room.

'William, I thought I'd better come to see if she was alright but I can't wake her.'

She started to shake.

'Don't be silly, she's probably just taken something to help her sleep.' He pushed passed Sylvia and went into the room. His Mother looked ashen.

'No surely not,' he thought. He felt sick with fear and anticipation. He walked to the bed and touched his mother's hand. It was cold and limp.

'Oh Christ no!' He threw his head on his mothers chest and started to sob. 'Get a doctor quick!' He turned his tear-stained face towards Sylvia, but he knew a doctor would be useless. His mother was dead.

Rosemary suggested they contacted their own doctor. Dr Murray arrived after about fifteen minutes and was taken upstairs to Martha's room.

'Did she feel unwell at all?' he asked William.

'Well she had a bad stomach after dinner last night and she said she'd take some medicine before she went to bed' William replied.

The doctor examined Martha's body and said he was almost certain she'd died of a heart attack.

'That's nonsense! My mother never suffered with her heart. Although she was seventy, she was fit!' He held onto the bedroom chair shaking a little.

'You see Mr Hounslow, anyone can have a heart attack, you don't necessarily have to have heart trouble and your mother was elderly.'

'I can't understand it' Williams voice faltered as he put his head in his hands.

'Come on old chap, you look as if you could do with a stiff drink' and George led him out of the room.

'She doesn't seem to have vomited' the doctor turned to Rosemary. 'So I think it was only a mild stomach upset. she may have thought the pains in her chest were indigestion but they could have been early indications of a heart attack. Normally I would sign the death certificate, but as she is not my patient, I'd better send an Officer from the Coroners Department.'

'Is there really any need to?' Rosemary asked quickly' I wouldn't want any bad publicity for the hotel.'

'I can appreciate that, but it's normal practice and it

might put the son's mind at rest. If I could use your telephone?'

'Oh yes of course' said Rosemary, 'It's downstairs.'

'And if you could lock this room and make sure no one enters until they arrive.'

Rosemary consented and went to get the keys.

* * *

They all just had coffee and toast for breakfast and then went into the lounge. Dave stood by the window with Peter.

'Of course he'll have a bob or two now, William you know. She had shares in everything. I might suggest he invests a bit in a little business I've got my eye on.'

'I wouldn't mention anything Dave. William is very cut up.'

* * *

'Of course she never liked me,' said Sylvia, 'but I'd never wished her any harm. It's odd though, I thought she'd go on forever.'

'Well one never knows, live each day like it's your last that's what I always say. When Mavis moans at me about my fishing. Who knows what will happen tomorrow.'

'Oh for God's sake, shut up all of you!' screamed

Mavis. 'Can't you see what poor William is going through, he was very close to his mother. You all make me sick!' and she stormed out of the room.

* * *

Rosemary and George were drinking coffee in the kitchen.

'Do you know George, I hate to sound callous, but if it was something that Martha ate, we'll have the Health and Safety Inspectors here and they could close us down!'

'Don't start getting panicky Rosemary, you don't know yet.'

'But we've worked so hard to make this a success, I'd just die if we lost it all. I love it here, I could never go back.'

'You're getting too worked up. Don't jump the gun till we know something more definite.'

Just then Mary came into the kitchen. She started to cry.

'I've been a wicked girl, Ma'am' she said 'I've killed that poor old lady. I didn't mean to. Oh what and I going to do? Father Murphy will not forgive me this time.' She was sobbing hysterically.

Rosemary slapped her face and she stopped suddenly.

'I'm sorry Mary, but I had to do that. George go and get her a brandy quickly.'

Mary sat down on the kitchen chair and sipped the brandy.

'It tastes awful,' she sobbed.

'I know, but it will do you good. Now tell us slowly and carefully what you're talking about Mary.'

'Well I only wanted to make her ill. She's always having a go at me. Nothing I do is right. 'Don't do this Mary, the potatoes are wrong Mary!' She makes my life a misery.'

'Well I know Lil can be a bit trying,' George added.

'Anyway, I only wanted to make her ill. I didn't really mean to . . . . .'

'Well Lil has only got a stomach upset, she'll probably be in tomorrow.'

'Yes but the lady upstairs has died. She must have got hold of one of my bad mussels, but I don't know how.'

'What bad mussels?' George asked. 'Start from the beginning Mary.'

'Could I have another brandy please Sir?'

'Not till you've told us what happened!'

'Well you see, Mrs Burridge's always giving me little lessons on cooking and when she was boiling the mussels she explained that only those that had opened were fit to eat and the others were bad for you and had to be thrown away. 'She stopped to blow her nose on her apron and then continued. 'Well, I got the unopened ones out of the bin and prized them open with a knife. Well me and Mrs Burridge have our meal after the guests, as you know Ma'am, so I put two of the bad mussels on her plate. Well, I don't know how the lady upstairs had a bad mussel, but it's killed her and it'll probably kill Mrs Burridge. They'll lock me away! Oh, what will I do?' She started to sob again.

'The best thing for you to do at the moment Mary is go home,' said Rosemary. 'George and I will be able to manage today, we'll see you tomorrow and we'll have another chat.'

Mary got her coat and George ran her home.

When he returned it was about mid morning, Rosemary was on the phone.

'Well thank you Mr Burridge, I'm glad she's feeling better, I'll see you tomorrow. No there's no need for her to come in tonight, we'll' manage.'

'How is she?' asked George, as he hung his coat on the hall stand.

'Fine, it seems,' said Rosemary, 'although she was feeling dreadful last night, she's perked up and had a bit of breakfast.'

'Mind you, Lil's built like a cart horse, she'd get over anything.

'Yes, but I had mussels in the market one day, do you remember George? I must have had a bad one and I felt dreadful, but it did pass after a few hours.'

'Oh well, we'll have to wait for the results of the doctors tests.'

'Anyway, let's go and see how the others are.' They went into the lounge.

Dave came up and put his arm around Rosemary.

'Are you alright old gal? You look done in!'

'Shock to us all,' said Simon. 'What does the doctor think it is?'

'He thinks it was a heart attack bought on by a stomach upset.' said George, 'but he doesn't sound too sure.'

'Where's Peter and Celia?'

'Well she's feeling sick, so Peter's taken her upstairs.'

'Oh no, not another one,' sighed Rosemary. 'I must go and see her.'

She knocked on the bedroom door.

'Come in.'

'How's Celia?'

Peter pointed to Celia who was being violently sick in the adjoining bathroom sink.

'I just don't believe this' said Rosemary, 'Shall I get a doctor?'

'I know I'm a little worried about her.'

After a few minutes Celia came out.

'I'm okay. Don't worry, it's not gastric. I was going to tell you alone Peter, but while Rosemary's here I'll tell you both, I'm expecting a baby.'

'Oh how wonderful Darling!' Peter hugged her.

'Oh I'm so pleased for you Celia, and so pleased for myself that it's nothing you've eaten.'

'I won't tell the others yet though' said Celia.'I feel the timings bad with William being so upset and everything.'

'Okay' said Peter 'We'll keep it to ourselves. Now you have a rest my darling and I'll pop and see you later!'

'Mary,' said Lil as 'I expect to have some visitors you have a rest my darling and I'll be along in just a minute.'

CHAPTER EIGHT

Accidents can happen

About three o'clock in the afternoon Rosemary went to find George. He was in the garden.

'I've had a phone call from the Coroner's office, he'll be here shortly.'

'Well I shall be glad to get the body out of the hotel' George said. 'It's a bit creepy really.'

'Do you think we ought to tell him or Dr Murray about the bad mussels?' asked Rosemary.

'Well not just yet, I mean, Mary says the bad mussels were put on Lil's dish and kept in the kitchen and not taken into the dining room at all. So if Martha did eat a bad mussel it could have been just coincidence, or it might be the wine sauce that was poured over them that didn't agree with her, or maybe it wasn't a stomach upset at all and just her heart as Dr Murray indicated.

'Yes, I suppose you're right' said Rosemary.

'I won't mention it to them at the moment.'

'I don't think we'll tell Lil either about Mary giving

her a bad mussel, because it could make things between them worse. Though I shall have to warn Mary, if she ever does anything so stupid again, I'll have to let her go and tell her mother.'

'Well I suppose we could give her another chance. I think she's learnt her lesson' George replied. 'Anyway we'll have a quiet cup of tea before this coroner chap arrives' and he went to put the kettle on.

At about four o'clock in the afternoon, a gentleman by the name of Mr Birkin arrived from the Coroners office and introduced himself to Rosemary and George. They showed him to the room where Martha's body was.

'I believe the son is staying with you, would it be possible to have a word with him?' Mr. Birkin enquired.

'Well he's asleep at the moment, the doctor gave him a sedative, but I can wake him' said George.

'No, don't bother him, it isn't that important. I can speak to him after the post mortem examination. Dr Murray seems convinced that it was a heart attack and I have no reason to doubt him, he's a very competent man. Still as she was on holiday here it is the normal procedure. I gather she wasn't just a guest?'

'No' said Rosemary. 'We've got some friends staying and she was the mother of one of our friends.'

Just as that moment William staggered into the room looking rather docile.

'William, you look absolutely dreadful, what are you doing out of bed?' Rosemary said.

Mr Birkin came round and offered his hand to William.'I gather you are the son of the deceased' he said solemnly. 'I was just saying to Mr and Mrs Richards, we'll have to take your mothers body for a post mortem.'

'I don't want her cut about' stammered William, and tears welled in his eyes.

'I can assure you sir, it is performed by highly trained doctors in a dignified manner.'

William fell back into the bedroom chair with his head in his hands.

'I'll take him to his room.' Rosemary led him out. The Coroner turned to George 'I take it, it was the son who refused to believe the late Mrs Hounslow had had a heart attack, so he should be pleased that we are doing a post mortem.'

'Well he was very close to his mother' George snapped.

'Oh yes, I see, well . . . . it's only a job to us, I hope you can appreciate that.' And he departed with two other men, with Martha's body.

'How is he?' asked George as Rosemary came out of William's room.

'He's sleeping. I think that sedative is taking effect now.'

'Very abrupt those chaps, aren't they?' said George.

'Well it's just a job to them.'

'Mmm, I suppose you're right. By the way, where is everyone?'

'Well under the circumstances they said they would

all go into town and eat, Celia and Mavis are still here. Mavis is concerned about William.'

'I suppose Sylvia doesn't give a damn' George said angrily.

'Well you know she's never really cared for Martha.'

'I know, but you'd think she'd be with William at his time of grief.'

'She said she couldn't do any good here and he'd probably sleep for hours, so she's gone with the others.'

'Bloody typical!' said George.

※ ※ ※

It was later that night when William awoke to find Mavis sitting by the side of his bed. 'Hello darling' he said.

'How red and swollen his eyes look' thought Mavis as she stroked his hair.

'I'm so glad you're here Mavis' he said sleepily. 'I do love you so.' And he fell back to sleep.

The next morning, after a long rest due to the sedatives William had taken, and a good breakfast inside him. He looked and felt almost human again. They all gave their condolences but nobody knew what to say really, and they felt awkward. Consequently they all seemed to disappear to do various things after breakfast.

Rosemary tried to catch up on jobs that she had neglected over the last few days, and was busy checking the accounts when the phone range about mid morning. It was the Coroners office.

Rosemary asked if it would be possible for them to make arrangements to have the body sent back to the Midlands, as Mr Hounslow was feeling better and was anxious to start funeral arrangements.

'Well that won't be possible at the moment Mrs Richards.' the Coroner replied. 'There seems to be some sort of confusion on how exactly she died and we need to do further tests. I should be contacting you within the next couple of days or so, as soon as the tests are complete.'

'Well I'll be available said Rosemary nervously.'Goodbye.'

'George, oh George, where are you?' she ran shouting down the hall way.

CHAPTER NINE

An Inspector calls

Inspector Trafford sat at his desk at the Torquay Police Department. He was a middle aged man in his fifties, receding slightly and rather plump. Despite this, he always wore a smartly cut suit and a dickie bow and looked rather dapper despite his build.

He'd just plugged the kettle in at the side of his desk for his morning tea, when Sergeant Roper came in with a paper cup in his hand.

'I don't know how you can drink that stuff Roper, what the inside of your stomach is like I dread to think!'

'It's not so bad when you get used to it,' Roper laughed. 'I'm going to get a bacon sandwich, do you fancy one sir?'

'We haven't got time now, I've told you to have breakfast before you come in. I've had a call from Mr. Birkin at the Coroners Office. He's just done a post mortem on an elderly lady and he's found a large quantity of drugs in the body. Thinks it might be a bit suspicious. He wants us to have a chat with him.'

Inspector Trafford finished his tea and they left with Sergeant Roper thinking he'd have had time for that bacon sandwich after all.

Mr. Birkin led them into the mortuary. It was cold and clinical.

'I'll never get used to these places' Sergeant Roper thought to himself.

'Alright' said Inspector Trafford as they came to Martha's body. 'What's the gen on this one then?'

'Well, Dr. Murray the local GP suspected a heart attack. He wasn't really wrong to do so. The lady was seventy and although she was reasonably fit all the symptoms pointed to it. We only did a post mortem as a standard procedure, as she was just visiting Torquay and she wasn't Dr. Murray's patient. As she had complained of a stomach upset I decided to check the contents of her stomach and I found a large quantity of the heart drug, Digoxin.'

'Enough to kill her?' asked Inspector Trafford.

'Oh most definitely. The usual dosage is one tablet a day. I'd say that she'd taken the equivalent of about thirty by the amount of the drug I've found in the bloodstream.'

'I've heard of Digoxin, my mother takes that.' said Inspector Trafford.

'Well Digoxin makes the heat beat faster.'

'So what would happen?' enquired Sergeant Roper.

'With one or two tablets it enables the heart to beat

at a regular pace but the amount she had taken, approximately thirty tablets, it would beat at such a fast speed it would burn itself out like a car engine.

'Mmm, not a very pleasant way to go. said Inspector Trafford straightening his dickie bow.

'Apart from that, she seemed to be in good health.' said Mr. Birkin.

'Do you think it could have been an accident Sir?' said Sergeant Roper, turning to Inspector Trafford.

'Well I suppose you could take a few extra by mistake, but certainly not that many.'

'She could have taken the overdose on purpose.' said Sergeant Roper.

'Quite possible, that assumption, she must have known the strength of the tablets and that such a large amount would have definitely been fatal.' added Mr. Birkin

'Mmm.' Inspector Trafford stroked his chin.

'What's the problem?' enquired Mr. Birkin.

'Well I was just thinking. Look at this ladies hair and nails. It looks like she has been a regular visitor to the hairdressers and beauty salons.'

'Fancy you knowing about that Sir!' Roper joked.

'Well my wife spends enough of my hard earned money in them. No, the point I was trying to make is that most people who commit suicide are depressed or in trouble and the first thing to go is their appearance. They just can't be bothered to take care of themselves.'

'Well I'm going to contact the lady's own doctor in the

Midlands later, a Dr. Lloyd. I'll ring you as soon as I have any information.'

'Okay that will be fine. I've got a talk this afternoon in a local school, but I'll be back at the station later.'

* * *

Mavis, Simon, Celia and Peter were all having afternoon tea in the lounge.

'Well I think we all ought to go home.' said Mavis.

'Nonsense!' chirped Simon. 'What's the use of cutting short our holiday! It can't bring the old gal back you know, and I for one haven't done half the fishing trips I planned.'

'You're so callous Simon! You've got no feeling at all.'

'If it had been me that had died, say I'd drowned in the river, she wouldn't have cut her holiday short.'

'Yes, life must go on you know.' Peter tapped Mavis's hand. 'Anyway, I've got a bit of good news to tell you, though it's a bit of an inappropriate time.' He put an arm around Celia and drew her to him. 'Celia's pregnant!' He said proudly.

'How marvellous!' exclaimed Mavis.

'Congratulations. Well done the pair of you. This calls for a proper drink.' Simon beamed. 'Come along Peter.'

'I'm so pleased for you' Mavis turned to Celia.

'I'm a little old you know, I'm thirty-four.'

'Well that's not old and they have got all those tests now to see if the baby's okay, and you don't smoke or drink. I'm sure you'll be fine.' said Mavis cheerfully.

'What about a little trip out. We could look at some baby things.'

'Isn't it supposed to be bad luck to buy anything?' asked Celia.

'Oh that's a load of cods wallop! Stupid superstition!' Mavis assured her. Just then William came in.

'How are you?' Mavis said looking longingly into his eyes.

'I'm not too bad now.'

'Well I've got something to tell you.' 'Oh no Mavis!' Celia said quickly.

'What are you talking about?'

'Celia's expecting a baby!'

'Well that's marvellous, you shouldn't have been worried about telling me. I could do with a bit of good news.'

'We're just off out now,' Celia said 'I'll go and fetch my coat' She went out.

'I was wondering if we could have some time together?' William whispered.

'I'm just going shopping with Celia, but I'll see you later.' She went out hesitantly.

* * *

The phone rang in Inspector Trafford's office.

'Sergeant Roper here. Oh hello Mr. Birkin. No he's not here at the the moment. He's still at the school I think . . . . Oh really that's interesting. Well I'm sure he'll want to go and see them . . . . Yes, I'll tell him as soon as he gets back . . . Not all . . . . Goodbye.'

'Well fancy that!' he thought to himself, as he put down the receiver.

Inspector Trafford's car pulled onto the driveway of the Sherwell Hotel. The tyres crunched on the gravel.

'I wish you wouldn't drive so fast Roper' I dread to think what damage you've done to my tyres.' He looked stern.

'Nice looking place isn't it Sir?' Roper quickly changed the subject.

They got out of the car and Inspector Trafford looked up at the house. 'They don't build houses like this anymore. Solid and full of character. Not like the rubbish you find on these modern estates. They're all like a lot of matchboxes all on top of one another.'

Rosemary came to the door rather anxiously.

'Looks like she's expecting us.' Roper said as they walked up the drive.

'Good morning Mrs Richards. I've just been admiring your hotel.'the Inspector looked around.

'Yes, we like it, thankyou. The Coroner told us you would be coming but I don't know why?' She sounded anxious, her voice faltered.

'Inspector Trafford introduced himself and Sergeant

Roper. He explained he just wanted a few words.

Rosemary led them into the lounge. A pleasant bright room, with flowered curtains around the bay, in shades of pink and green. There was a floral suite to match with large comfortable cushions. It looked fresh and welcoming.

When they were seated she called Mary and asked for coffee to be served.

＊ ＊ ＊

Inspector Trafford looked at the woman facing him. He had always had a thing about redheads. His wife had been red in her younger days, but was now a sandy grey colour.

Rosemary's hair was a rich auburn, her complexion wasn't as pale as most red heads, but she did have a few freckles, which she loathed, but the inspector thought them most attractive.

She had large round blue eyes that looked almost childlike.

'That doesn't sound like a Devon accent' said Sergeant Roper.

'Oh don't say I sound like a 'Brummie'' Rosemary smiled, relaxing a little. 'We've only been here six months but we love it.'

'A lot of people who come to live in Devon nearly always stay' said Inspector Trafford.

'That's why I was a little concerned at you coming to

see us Inspector. We've worked so hard to make a success of this hotel. We're making new friends and we wouldn't want any bad publicity.'

'Look, don't worry. We'll be as discreet as possible.' Inspector Trafford assured her as he patted her hand.

'What a kind man' she thought 'and what a cute bow tie.'

At that moment George came into the room and after the usual introductions he sat down. Mary brought in the coffee.

'Shall I get another cup for Mr Richards?' she asked.

'No, I'm okay thanks Mary' George answered.

'Now then' said Inspector Trafford 'let's get down to business. I believe Mrs Hounslow's son is staying with you?'

'Yes' answered Rosemary, 'But he's gone for a walk on the beach with the others. He's taken it very badly and hasn't been too well lately.'

'That's understandable' said Inspector Trafford. 'I can see him later.'

'Well is there a problem?' George asked. 'Dr. Murray seemed to think she'd had a heart attack.'

'Well the thing is sir,' Inspector Trafford fiddled with his bow tie, 'the coroner found a large quantity of a heart drug Digoxin in the deceased's stomach containing easily enough to kill her.'

'I didn't know she suffered with her heart' Rosemary said amazed.

'Precisely, she didn't!' said Sergeant Roper.

'Mr Birkin contacted her own doctor in the Midlands, a Dr. Lloyd, who confirmed he had never prescribed the drug Digoxin for her as she had never suffered with her heart.' Inspector Trafford added.

'Well how then . . . .?' Rosemary asked in amazement.

'Exactly!' said Inspector Trafford, stirring his coffee.

'Originally, we thought she was taking the drug and just overdosed by mistake, although it was hard to believe that someone could take such a large dose by mistake. Then we thought suicide.'

'Martha, commit suicide! Never in a month of Sundays!' George remarked.

'You knew the lady well then?' asked Inspector Trafford.

'We've know her for years. You see, Inspector, William and his wife Sylvia are good friends of ours. They came to stay with us along with some others and Martha came with them.' George informed Inspector Trafford.

'I wish it was suicide or an accident' said Rosemary. 'We couldn't stand any bad publicity for ourselves, or William. But I'll tell you Inspector, Martha Hounslow was a hard business woman who loved life. I can think of a number of people who she'd get rid of, but she'd never kill herself, I'm sure of that!'

'Then, there's only one explanation left' said Inspector Trafford, 'Martha Hounslow was murdered!'

Rosemary dropped her cup on the floor. 'I don't believe it' she stuttered. She looked pleadingly at

George who came and sat at her side.

'I know it puts Mr Richards and yourself in an awkward position, but there it is. If you could inform all your guests I shall be wanting to speak to them later and I'm afraid they will not be able to return to home at the moment.' He shook their hands and departed with Sergeant Roper.

Rosemary sobbed in George's lap. 'I knew she'd get this place off me somehow!'

'What are you talking about Rosemary?'

'Well . . . .er . . . What I mean is now she's dead, I know this sounds heartless George, but we could lose guests with all this publicity.'

'Look don't worry, we might get more, you know how some people can be. They'll want to visit the hotel where the murder took place.' He tried to laugh, but secretly he was as worried as Rosemary.

CHAPTER TEN

The suspects

They were all gathered in the lounge.

'Murdered eh! Well I say' Simon carefully cleaned his fishing rod. 'It's possible you know, I'd have like to have done her in myself sometimes!'

'Oh Simon!' Mavis twisted her handkerchief between · her fingers.

'Oh well it's a bit of excitement I suppose.'

'You won't think that when they start questioning us all. Once they get hold of something they don't let it lie and you realise that none of us will be allowed to leave until the matter is cleared up!' Peter looked serious.

'It doesn't bother me. I can get some extra fishing in.'

'Well in Celia's condition, I don't think she needs all this excitement it isn't good for her!' Peter added angrily.

'I'm okay darling I'm feeling much better now.' Celia put her hand on Peter's arm.

'Anyway, I don't know what you lot are worried

about. It's me and William who benefit, it's us they're going to be after.' Sylvia started to apply some powder from her compact.

'Where is William anyway? asked Simon.

'God knows. He keeps wondering off somewhere.'

Just then Rosemary came in with tea on a tray.

'We're just wondering how long we'll all have to stay here for,' said Mavis as she helped Rosemary with the tray.

'I don't know' said Rosemary. 'I wish it was all over and done with. It's bad for business, anyway the quicker he sees us all the quicker it will be over. He'll be here soon, so I've brought you all a drink.'

'An alcoholic beverage would have been more apt.' said Simon and he went out.

✳ ✳ ✳

With Rosemary's permission, Inspector Trafford and Sergeant Roper set up in the study when they arrived.

'Is the son back yet?' he asked Rosemary.

'He's just come in!'

'I'll tell you what, I'll have Mrs Sylvia Hounslow in first.'

Sylvia entered the room. she had on a well tailored pale blue suit that was rather tight in all the right places and her hair and make-up were exquisite as always.

'Looks a bit hard to handle' Inspector Trafford

thought to himself.

'Please take a seat Mrs Hounslow!' Sergeant Roper quickly moved forward to help her. She smiled at him.

'Thank you' she said. 'Oh please call me Sylvia, Inspector. Do you mind if I smoke?'

'Not at all.'

Sergeant Roper quickly came forward and lit her cigarette.

'I believe it was you who found the late Mrs Hounslow?'

'Well yes, I knocked on her door and there was no reply so I went in and I couldn't wake her.'

'Did you know she was dead?'

'Well not at first!'

'Can you think of anyone who would want to kill your mother-in-law, Mrs . . . . .er Sylvia!'

'Yes plenty . . . ' she said as she blew a circle of smoke in the air!

'Are you including yourself in that?' asked Inspector Trafford.

'Look Inspector, I never got on with her it was common knowledge. She never approved of me. I think she thought that her son could have done better and if it hadn't been for his business I think she would have liked us to have parted.'

'But she didn't like the possibility of divorce?'

'Precisely. She thought it would be bad for William's business image!'

'And did she help him out financially?'

'Well she'd given him a lump sum to get the business started and she also gave us a monthly allowance.'

'Quite a generous woman then?' remarked Sergeant Roper.

'There was method in her madness. She had half shares in the business as William couldn't make a major financial decision without her permission and the allowance she gave us was a pittance!'

Inspector Trafford thought that was probably an exaggeration. Most people could possibly have managed quite well.

'And the night before she died?'

'Well after dinner she complained of stomach pains. Rosemary suggested getting a doctor but she said she'd be okay and she went to bed.'

'Mmm I see. Well that'll be all for now. Thank you Mrs Hounslow.'

Sergeant Roper jumped up to open the door for her.

'I've told you to call me Sylvia' she winked at them both as she left.

'A very attractive woman!' sighed Sergeant Roper.

'Yes, but rather made-up I felt! I should imagine she's led the son a bit of a life! There was certainly no love lost for her mother-in-law, and now Mrs Hounslow will come into all the money I suppose!'

'Well it's certainly a motive to kill for money.'

'I think we'll have the son in now.' said Inspector Trafford.

* * *

William Hounslow entered the room and shook hands with the two men.

'I'm sorry I kept you waiting, I had to go and get my car from the garage.'

'Are you feeling better now Sir?' Inquired Inspector Trafford.

'Yes, thankyou. I know a lot of people think it's weak for a man to show his feelings, but I loved my mother. I know she had her faults but she was good to me.'

'I can understand that' said Inspector Trafford. 'My own mother is eighty five years of age and I still have to watch what I say, but I think the world of her. Now sir, if you could tell me what happened on the evening before your mother died.'

'Well before dinner Dave told me that someone had scratched my car, I don't mind telling you Inspector, I was upset.'

'Yes, they're nice cars those Jaguars' said Sergeant Roper. 'I wouldn't mind one myself.'

'It was a long deep scratch all along the wheel arch.'

'Kids I suppose' suggested Roper.

'Anyway, I didn't eat much dinner, I felt bad about the car.'

'Your mother was okay at dinner?'

'I'll say. She even finished my starter.'

'And after dinner?'

'Well afterwards when the others were playing cards,

she said she felt ill.'

'Why didn't you insist she had a doctor?' asked the Inspector.

'You couldn't insist my mother did anything she didn't want to, Inspector. Anyway, she always had a complete medicine chest with her wherever she went. She said she'd take some of her own stomach medicine.'

'Mmm I can see that certain old ladies rely on their own judgement as to what they need. They don't always trust doctors and of course it wouldn't have been her own doctor that would have come.' said Inspector Trafford.

'She gave me some stomach medicine the other day and it was good stuff, it settled my stomach, so I suppose I thought she'd be okay. When the doctor said it was her heart, I knew he was wrong. But this overdose of Digoxin. My mother would never have had any such drug.'

'And you don't think she would have got it from somewhere and taken an overdose?'

'Never, I can tell you she wouldn't have committed suicide I'm certain of it. Her personality was too strong she wasn't that type.'

'So that brings us back to the fact that it was administered to her somehow.'

'But who would want to murder my mother?' William looked incredulously.

'Your wife thinks it's quite possible.'

'Well Sylvia didn't like my mother and vice versa.'

'I understand you will benefit considerably Mr Hounslow?'

'Well my mother did have several thousands invested. I certainly won't be short.'

'Your wife was complaining that the existing allowance wasn't very much.'

'It's quite adequate. My wife is just a spendthrift, she spends pounds on designer clothes and special skin preparations. She's terrible at managing money.'

'I suppose she'll have a lot more to spend now?' inquired Roper.

'Not if I have anything to do with it she won't, and I'll tell you this Inspector, I'd rather have my mother here than all the money in the world.' He moved uneasily in his chair.

'Yes I believe you would' thought Inspector Trafford to himself.

'Well thank you Mr Hounslow. That'll be all for now.'

'Okay Inspector. By the way have you any idea how long this will take? Only I would like to get my mother's body back home and start funeral arrangements?'

'I can appreciate that sir, but I also hope you realise that we have a job to do and I'm sure you'll want to know how your mother got hold of the Digoxin or if anyone gave it to her.'

'Well yes I want the matter cleared up, but do you really think it was murder Inspector? I mean it's a bit far fetched.'

'Well unless she took an overdose herself which

everybody seems to think she wouldn't, that is all we can assume at the moment!'

'Well I suppose you're right.' William left the room in a sort of daze.

'Mmm' Inspector Trafford stroked his chin. 'Seems to have been very fond of his mother.'

'Could be an act though Sir?' Roper intervened.

'Yes, possible. He's a business man so he must be fairly hard and astute and yet . . . .'

'Well what about Mrs Hounslow?'

'Sylvia you mean!' smiled Inspector Trafford. 'I think she'd be capable of anything if she thought she would benefit.'

'Yes Sir, but she doesn't seem as if she will from what her husband said' added Roper.

'I think sparks will fly there. Now who's next. Mmm Mr and Mrs Turley I think!'

'Do you want to see them both together?'

'No I'll see Mr Turley first. If you could ask for him on your way out Roper.'

* * *

Simon Turley entered the room.

'Good morning Sir. I just need to ask you a few questions, it won't take long.'

'Not at all Inspector!! We've got to help our Police that's what I always say. Ask me what you want as long as it won't take too long, only I'm going to look at some rods later.'

'Now sir, I believe you knew the late Mrs Hounslow.'

'Only through William and Sylvia. Went everywhere with them she did. You wouldn't catch me taking my mother-in-law with me I can tell you. Under the thumb he was. Mind you, Sylvia never liked her. Trim little thing ain't she? Do you do any fishing Inspector?'

'Occasionally sir.'

'Well really now!' I was wondering do you know . . . '

'If you could just stick to the point.'

'Oh yes . . . . er . . . sorry.'

'Mr Hounslow tells me his car was badly scratched before dinner a few evenings ago?'

'Oh yes. Still if he will have those bloody expensive motors. Serves him right.'

'Do you drive Sir?'

'No came down on the train we did, quieter and safer. Mavis would like a car, but I told her we couldn't afford one.'

'Yes . . . sir . . . precisely, and is there anything you can tell us about anything unusual that happened on the night Martha Hounslow died?'

'Well I wish I could Inspector, sounds a bit exciting doesn't it? A real who dunnit. No, the old gal had a bad stomach and went to bed and then the next day. 'bingo' she's gone. Of course Inspector, he'll be loaded now you know, she had thousands. He was in a right old state as well. He should have pulled himself together and decided what he was going to do with all that money.

Mavis kept saying how sorry she felt for him. Sorry, the lucky blighter, I wish I had his money.'

'Now sir do you know of anybody who would want to see Mrs Hounslow dead?'

'Plenty would. Nasty old cow. Never like her and she didn't like me you know! and I've heard her having a go at Rosemary. I don't know why she had her here. And old Peter, well he didn't get on with her at all! Even said to me he'd like to kill her.'

'Really sir? When was that?'

'Oh one day when we went to Dartmoor. She'd probably said something to upset him. Nasty mouth she'd got on her.'

'Well thank you sir' Inspector Trafford got up. 'That'll be all for now.'

'Glad I've been of help Inspector, call on me anytime.'

'Could you show your wife in now sir.'

'Certainly inspector. She'll be no help though. Waste of time. These women, no logic you know.' He left the room.

Inspector Trafford sat down exhausted. 'Thank God for that' he thought. He could still hear Simons voice as he walked down the hallway.

'Mavis get a move on, the Inspector wants to see you.'

Sergeant Roper came in.

'We'll just interview Mrs Turley and then we'll call it a day.'

Mavis came in and sat down. She looked nervous and a little pale.

'Can I get you a drink or anything?' Inspector Trafford enquired.

'No thank you' said Mavis politely. 'My husband said you wanted to see me.'

'Yes, just routine enquiries. Now Mrs Turley, in your own words, I'd like your opinion of Mrs Hounslow and also if you noticed anything unusual on the day she died.'

Mavis smiled, she was quite pleased someone had asked her opinion about something.

'Well Sylvia, I know she can fuss about herself' she began.

'No . . . Mrs Turley, we mean the late Mrs Hounslow' said Sergeant Roper.

'Oh how silly of me . . . do forgive me. Well she could be a bit stern at times, but she was a very good mother to William, she gave him everything.'

'And how did you get on with her?'

'Well she never did me any harm although she could be nasty to the others.'

'Your husband doesn't seem to have got on with her!'

A look of indifference passed over her face.

'Oh he doesn't get on with anybody unless they're interestered in fishing.'

'Your husband seems to think she was rather abrupt with Mrs Richards and also Mr Bellamy.'

'Oh well I must admit she has been a bit funny with Rosemary, but I didn't think Peter . . . But then she was getting on a bit and I suppose old ladies do get a bit cantankerous.'

'So in your opinion do you think anyone would want to murder her?'

'Oh goodness no, inspector.'

'Now can you tell me what happened on the evening before?'

'Well there was the touble over William's car. He was very upset, such a nice car. All the men went to look at it and then we had our evening meal. Of course, we had mussels and those can upset your stomach if you're not careful and Martha had William's becuase he didn't feel like them and then after dinner, later in the evening Martha was taken poorly and went to bed. Poor William has been very upset by all this, I do hope it can be cleared up quickly. Is that all Inspector only I've got to sort some things out for my husband?'

'Yes, I think so. Thank you Mrs Turley.'

'Thank you both' Mavis smiled at them and left the room.

'What's she thanking us for?' asked Roper.

'I shouldn't think she gets a good deal from the man in her life. She's thanking us for being reasonably nice to her.'

'Poor old thing' laughed Roper.

Inspector Trafford turned to Roper and asked him to get Mrs Richards before they left.

'Oh god I thought we were finished' Roper thought slightly depressed. 'Okay I'll get her for you.'

Rosemary came in a little flushed she had that glow

to her face that redheads sometimes get when they're warm. She'd got some spray polish in one hand and a duster in the other.

'I'm sorry about this' said the Inspector 'Just a few things I want to go over with you and we'll call it a day.' He felt a bit guilty that he had upset her routine.

'That's alright Inspector. We ought to have a cleaner really but it's extra money you know.' She sat down glad of the break from her chores.

'What time was the evening meal served the night before?' inquired the Inspector.

'Oh about eight o'clock or a few minutes later, with everyone looking at the car it was delayed.'

'And what time did Mrs Hounslow complain of stomach pains?'

'Oh about ten o'clock I suppose. She decided to go to bed. It must have been about ten fifteen or ten thirty pm I'm not really sure.'

'And did you offer her any medicine when she wouldn't have a doctor?'

Rosemary looked amazed. 'She wouldn't have anything off me Inspector. She always had her own medicine supply with her. She was a bit fussy.'

'Are they still in her room?'

'Yes'

'Then I'd like to see them.'

Rosemary took them up to Martha's room. There was a box on her dressing table with every sort of medicine you could imagine. The Inspector and Roper sorted through them. Paracetamols, Codine, Cyclax powders, Milk of Magnesia, various bottle of cough medicine.

'I think we'll take these with us to get them checked Roper.'

'Okay sir, I'll pack them all up.'

'I trust no-one has been in the room?'

'Well it's been locked Inspector.'

'Yes well I think we'll have the lab boys over just to check everything out.' They left with the medicines.

As they walked down the drive to the car the Inspector turned to Roper 'I think I'll go home a bit early, give the wife a treat, you can take those into the lab.'

'Okay' said Roper.

He sat in the passenger seat as Roper drove a little too quickly, Inspector Trafford shut his eyes and started to think. After a few minutes he turned to Roper.

'Mr. Birkin told us Digoxin was quick to work, so I don't think it was administered in the evening meal at all, otherwise she'd have been dead before 10 o'clock.'

'So you think it was taken later?'

'Definitely. I think it points to being in the medicine. Now lets see, upset stomach, she'd take the Milk of Magnesia I suppose or perhaps indigestion tablets of some sort. Still we'll wait and see what the tests on the medicines are.'

Roper pulled up outside his house.

'I'll see you tomorrow then Roper.'

Inspector Trafford got out of the car and looked up

at the sky. 'I'll be able to have the deckchair out for half an hour' he thought 'And get that last bit of sun.'

* * *

The following morning Inspector Trafford had a call from the lab to say the tests were complete and they had got some information for him. When he arrived, the lab assistant sounded quite enthusiastic about his findings.

'We've tested all the medicines and found particles of the drug Digoxin in the Magnesia Triscillicate bottle. I should imagine the tablets were crushed to a fine powder and poured into the bottle.'

'What exactly is Magnesia Triscillicate?'

'Well it's just another name for Milk of Magnesia. It can be made up by a chemist or bought over the counter, it's very popular. Most people take it for upset stomachs.'

'So the murderer was just waiting until Mrs Hounslow had a bad stomach, she'd take the medicine and that would be that' Roper announced.

'Well yes, it's a very powerful drug. I should imagine if the tablets were crushed you could get quite a lot into a bottle.' said Peters the lab assistant. 'Look here's a tablet, it's very small you see, you could crush about ten to twelve in one teaspoon. He held a small tablet in the palm of his hand. 'She'd only have to take couple of spoonfuls and that would have been enough to kill her and she'd shake the bottle so the drug would have been dispersed. Even a small amount taken by someone without a bad heart would cause the heart to beat faster and bring on a heart attack.'

'Your results tie up with what the Coroner said, only we didn't know how the drug was administered. You have been a great help, thanks.' said Inspector Trafford shaking his hand.

That lunchtime Inspector Trafford and Sergeant Roper were having lunch in the pub.

'I think it was probably common knowledge that Mrs Hounslow had a medicine box' Roper mumbled as he bit into his cheese roll. 'What I can't understand is how did the murderer know she'd have an upset stomach and take it. What if someone else had been ill and she'd have offered them her medicine, they'd have died as well?'

'Well this is where the murderer would have had to make sure Martha Hounslow got sick before anyone else did. They had to be certain she'd take the medicine that night. Something must have been put in that evening meal to make her ill.'

'Well the people that would have any opportunity to mess with the food would be the kitchen staff and Mr and Mrs Richards.' Roper intervened.

'Mm I think we'll have to check the procedure on how the meals are served.' Inspector Trafford remarked.

Roper got up from his chair 'Another pint sir?'

'No thanks Roper and no more for you, we've got work to do.'

✳ ✳ ✳

µ'So you want to know about the evening meal?'George looked a little perplexed.

'Well yes, as much as you can recall Mr Richards.'

'Well lets see, we had Moules Marinére as a starter followed by lamb and veg and an apple pie to finish.'

'Sounds delicious.' said Roper.

'Are all the meals served in the kitchen and then brought in when the guests are seated?'

'Sometimes the starters are put out before the guests are actually seated, and if I remember rightly the starters were on the table for a while that evening as they were all outside looking at William's car.'

'Thanks' said the Inspector 'I'll have a word with the cook presently.'

'Old Lil eh! Well I'm not sure, if she's busy, doesn't like being disturbed when she's cooking.'

'I'll come in to see her in a few minutes then' said the Inspector. and George left.

'Mmm mussels a bit dicky for anyone's stomach.' Roper scratched his head

'Yes but the murderer had to make sure only Martha Hounslow was ill and no one else. It seems to me something must have been put into the starter. It could have been one of the guests as the starters were on the table unattended for a while. All the guests were seated for the other courses so it would have been risky to have put something in the food without them being noticed.'

'An ideal opportunity. Lucky for the murderer. The majority of them were looking at the car!' Roper grinned.

'Lucky opportunity. I wonder if the car was purposely scratched to get everyone out of the way to give the murderer more time. If so, we can eliminate those looking at the car. The ladies were still in here it could have been one of them or someone coming in from the car before the others. endless possibilities' said Inspector Trafford.

'But would any of them have motives? Mr and Mrs Hounslow benefit financially, but the others they had nothing to gain.'

'They may have done. We've got to look at these people more carefully. We don't know enough about any of them. We've still got more to interview. There's Celia and Peter Bellamy and Mr David Cranmore. I've heard that name before. I wonder if he's got a record? Anyway, we'll see the staff next.'

✳ ✳ ✳

Lil was stirring a large bowl of cake mixture and bits of it were sticking to her eyebrows and hair.

'The Inspector would like a word with you Lil' George said as he put his head round the door.

Lil stopped and wiped her face with her long white apron.

'Well I've only got a few minutes.'

'I won't keep you Mrs Burridge' said Inspector Trafford. 'Important business it is cooking. You know

Murder on the English Riviera

what they say, a way to a man's heart.'

Lil blushed. 'Quite so' she said and became more genial.

'Now I'd like to ask about the food on the evening before Mrs Hounslow died?'

'Now look here Inspector, nobody is as particular as me. You could eat food off this floor. I've been a cook at the Grand Hotel, never had a complaint . . .' She started to look very red in the face.

'I can assure you Mrs Burridge, I know of your culinary achievements. I am friend of the old chef at the Grand, Mr Burley, and he speaks very highly of you.' Mrs Burridge succumbed to this flattery.

'Well that's very nice to hear!'

'Is that one of your famous fruit cakes?' the Inspector pointed to a large cake on the table.

'Well it is actually . . . . Mary don't just stand there, cut these two gentlemen a slice of cake . . . and put the kettle on. Now Inspector, where were we?' she smiled.

'The evening meal.'

'Oh yes. Well we had Moules Marinére to start.'

'What is that exactly?'

'Well it's mussels in a white sauce, a speciality of mine' she said proudly. 'I'm very particular you know Inspector, I always make sure all the mussels have opened after boiling and I keep my sauce at exactly the right temperature.

If that woman was feeling ill it wasn't because of my cooking and no one else was ill except . . . .' she stopped.

'Yes what is it Mrs Burridge?'

'Well I was bad that night, in fact I couldn't come into work the next day. Funny that. I'm never ill. But it couldn't have been the mussels Inspector, they never upset me.'

'Did you and Mary have a meal?'

'Yes, we had ours when we'd finished working. The lamb and everything was cooked fine I can assure you Inspector.'

'Well thank you Mrs Burridge.'

They left presently with Mrs Burridge putting an extra piece of fruit cake wrapped in cling film into each of their pockets.

'That kitchen girl Mary looked a bit jumpy didn't she?' said Roper.

'Mmm yes. I'll speak to her later' the Inspector replied.

* * *

Mary shook like a leaf as she stood in front of the policeman.

'Now Mary just relax. Take a seat. 'The Inspector tried to reassure her.

'I'm a good Catholic girl I am. I wouldn't do any one any harm.'

'I'm sure you wouldn't Mary, we just want to ask you a few questions.'

She sat down twisting a handkerchief round and

round her fingers.

The Inspector nodded to Roper, and Roper asked 'Do you always carry the starters in before the meal Mary?'

'Yes Sir.'

'Now if we go into the dining room can you show me where Mrs Hounslow sat?'

As they went in Mary pointed to the middle seat on the right hand side of the table.

'Did she always sit there?' Roper asked.

'Yes, she said it was the only place that she didn't get a draught from the verandah window.'

'Now Mary think carefully, can you remember who was in here when you brought the starters in?'

'I think all the ladies sir, the men weren't there. There was Mrs Hounslow and her daughter-in-law who was reading and that nice lady, Mrs Turley, and Mrs Bellamy were on the veranda I think.'

'Okay Mary, that's fine. That'll be all for now.'

She scampered out like a frightened mouse.

CHAPTER ELEVEN

The proof of the pudding

The next day Sergeant Roper was sitting at his desk with a file in front of him but he didn't seem to be taking in what he was reading.

The Inspector plugged the kettle in.

'Fancy a cup of decent tea, Sergeant? I've got that home-made cake somewhere in this drawer that Mrs Burridge gave us!'

Sergeant Roper never answered for a few moments.

'None for me thanks.'

'There's something up here' thought the Inspector 'he never refuses food.'

'Aren't you feeling well?'

'I was just thinking sir, you know the son, William Hounslow, well he said he didn't want his starter and gave some mussels to his mother. Well do you think perhaps there was something on his mussels to make him ill and his mother took them by mistake?'

Well done Roper. Well done lad.'

'He always calls me lad' Roper laughed to himself 'and I'm nearly thirty-eight.'

'Well if that is the case, we could be barking up the wrong tree.'

The Inspector stood up and walked around the desk.

'Now let's work this out properly' he picked up his chalk and started to write on the blackboard. 'Well let's assume he could possibly have been the intended victim and Mrs Hounslow became ill by mistake.'

'The fatal dose of Digoxin was in Mrs Hounslow's medicine. They'd have to make sure he took it and nobody else.'

'Yes but she gave him some medicine the other day and he was okay then. So obviously the poison hadn't been put in the medicine then.'

'Maybe the murderer hoped he would take his mother's medicine again when the poison was in it.'

'Well this gets more complicated by the minute' Roper scratched his head 'And I've just thought, I'm sure someone said that chap Dave had some of William's mussels as well and he's okay.'

'Well whatever was put on the starter must have been something mild just enough to make someone slightly ill. If they'd been desperately ill an ambulance would have been called perhaps!'

'Yes, my guess is it could have been a drop of weedkiller or something like it, just enough to upset the stomach.'

Just then the phone rang.

'Hello, Inspector Trafford here. Oh hello Mrs Richards. Yes certainly we'll come . . . Oh you'd rather come here, that's fine. See you in an hour then.' He put the phone down. 'Seems rather anxious' the Inspector looked perplexed. 'Now I wonder what she wants to tell us?'

When Rosemary arrived, she related the incident to the two men about Mary making Lil ill with the unopened mussel.

'I wouldn't want the girl to get into any trouble Inspector, and there's no harm done, Lil's fine now. It's just what with Martha and everything, I thought you ought to know.'

'Do you Mrs Richards think there's any possibility of that one unopened mussels getting into the dining room where the guests were?'

'Frankly, no Inspector. Mary and and Lil's starters were kept well away from the others in the kitchen.'

'I don't suppose there's any connection there, she seems such a simple girl, but one never knows.'

'I wouldn't want her to know I'd been to see you' Rosemary looked pleadingly at the Inspector.

'I won't mention it unless it's relevant to the case' he reassured here. 'By the way Mrs Richards, I gather William gave his starter to his mother and Mr Cranmore?'

'Yes he was to upset over the car to finish his.'

'Well we believe something was put in someone's starter to make them ill. And this is strictly off the record, but still they've got to know soon. The drug Digoxin was found crushed up in the bottle of Mrs Hounslows stomach medicine.'

Rosemary suddenly shivered as if someone had walked over her grave.

'It's a frightening thought that someone in the hotel had been evil enough to work out such a plan. and you think it may have been in William's starter . . . . you mean . . . .'

'Yes, someone could have intended to murder him.'

Rosemary sat for a few moments. Listen Inspector, I'm a bit of an Agatha Christie fan and I don't want you to think I've been reading too many of her books . . . .'

Sergeant Roper laughed 'Have you got a clue for us Mrs Richards?'

'Oh it was just that I noticed Martha drinking all her white wine sauce with a spoon. Could it be whatever made her ill was in the sauce and not in any of the mussels?'

'That thought did occur to me also, Mrs Richards. A drop of something on one mussel would have tasted bitter, but in a white wine sauce, the taste would have been masked.'

'So you didn't mind me mentioning it?'

'Not at all and anything else you may be able to remember, please don't hesitate to contact us.'

'Oh I will Inspector, you can be sure of that.'

They saw Rosemary out, and she seemed a lot happier than when she arrived.

'Do you think that Mary is involved at all?' asked Roper.

'I don't think so, but one never knows. All we seem to know at the moment is how, but not who or why. Still I think we'd better keep an eye on Mr Hounslow just in case he was the intended victim and the murderer tries again.'

'Of course, the only one that would benefit would be his dear wife.'

CHAPTER TWELVE

The plot thickens

The following day, Inspector Trafford went back to the Sherwell to continue with his investigations. He asked to speak to Dave.

'Oh good morning. Mr David Cranmore?'

'Good morning. My word, nobody's called me David in years. I feel much happier with Dave if you don't mind.'

He sat down in front of the Inspector and Roper. 'He was a dapper little fellow' the Inspector thought 'but a bit of a Jack the lad.'

'Now Mr Cranmore, as you know, these investigations are about the death of Mrs Hounslow and the events leading up to her death. So if you could tell us as much as you can remember.'

'Well I'll do my best Inspector' Dave sat down and lit a cigarette.

'Now did you know the deceased very well?'

'Well only as far as she was William's mother. She

was a nasty piece of work, although having a mother like that you'd never be short of money. He was a lucky chap really!'

'Do you envy him then?' asked Roper.

'Well funnily enough no. I mean I envy his money, clothes and posh cars, but you know I think he's led quite a boring life. Now me, I like to be out and about selling. I've done it all my life, market stalls, suitcase on the road side, I mean I don't suppose I should be telling you this.'

'We're not really bothered whether you've got a licence or not, it's not our department, now if you were involved in stolen goods . . . . that would be a different story.'

'I wouldn't touch 'em Inspector, they'd be more trouble than they're worth.'

'I doubt that' the Inspector thought to himself.

'I don't suppose you gentlemen would be interested in some nice watches, good quality . . . . If you want to know the time ask a policeman eh!' Dave chuckled.

'I don't think so sir . . . . Now if we could get back to Mrs Hounslow. Do you know of anyone who might want to kill her?'

'I should think that most people would.'

'And what makes you think that?'

'Well she interfered in everyone's business. Even old Peter said he hated her guts.

'Really, now that's interesting.'

'Oh look Inspector, just a figure of speech. He didn't

mean it.' Dave wished he'd never opened his mouth.

'Well he must have said it for some reason' said Roper.

'I think she was just interfering in his private business. I'd have said the same thing myself.'

'So you can't think of anything else?'

'No, and look Inspector, I wouldn't like Peter to think I'd said anything. Honour amongst thieves and all that you know.'

He went out uneasily.

* * *

Sylvia grabbed Peter's arm as he walked out on to the terrace.

'How's Celia feeling? her voice was sarcastic as usual.

'She's fine thanks, a bit of morning sickness but I suppose that's to be expected.'

'Of course, I suppose you won't be getting all your marital rights, she'll be worried about harming the baby?'

'I can wait!' Peter jumped to his defence.

'Well I'm always here you know.'

Peter looked her up and down. Yes he still fancied Sylvia, he could have made love to her there and then but he would have to try and stop himself. He didn't have a lot of will power. He walked towards her and stroked her breast she was just about to respond when he pulled himself away.

'You're going to be a father for God's sake – act responsibly' he thought to himself.

'Sorry Sylvia, it's no good. Anyway, I've got to go and see that Inspector chap.' He turned abruptly and left.

Peter sat opposite Inspector Trafford and Sergeant Roper and answered the usual questions.

'And how did you get on with the deceased?' Inquired Inspector Trafford.

'Well I didn't really know her that well.'

'I gather she didn't approve of your friendship with Sylvia Hounslow?'

'I don't see why not!' Peter tried not to fidget in his chair but he felt distinctively uncomfortable. 'We were only friends, nothing more.'

'Isn't it true then Mr Bellamy, that you'd said you could have killed Martha Hounslow and you hated her guts?'

'I can't recall saying that, who told you that?'

'Well I can't disclose any names. Perhaps your wife can help us.'

'Now look, I don't want Celia brought into this, especially in her condition.'

'Oh yes, congratulations, I've got two myself' said Roper.

'Thank you . . . er Sergeant' He turned back to Inspector Trafford. 'Look Inspector, my wife doesn't know anything.'

'And neither do you by the sounds of it.'

'I have told you all I know!'

'This is a murder investigation if you hadn't noticed. I suggest you go away Mr Bellamy and think seriously about anything you have to tell me. I'd like to see you wife now.'

'If anything happens to her or the baby because you've upset her, you'll have me to reckon with. I don't want her knowing about Sylvia.'

'I thought there was nothing to know!'

'There isn't' he said firmly as he left the room.

Celia was quite pretty with her dark black curls and she had that bloom most pregnant women get even though she was in the early stages.

'Good day Mrs Bellamy, how are you feeling?'

'Fine thank you' she smiled.

'Now we won't keep you long, just a few questions. Now I've asked this several times before to the others, do you know of anyone that could have killed Mrs Hounslow?'

'Well, she wasn't really liked by anyone, but murder, I don't think anyone here would be capable of that but I suppose you never know really do you? Peter never seemed to like her, although I don't think she'd ever done any harm to him. My husband's always been friendly and got on with most people, all my friends adore him.'

'Er yes quite so . . . Now Mrs Bellamy, can you tell us anything about what happened before you all sat down to eat on the night she died?'

'Well let's see, that was the night William's car was damaged. Well I was on the terrace with Martha. I think she was knitting. Mavis had shown me an article in a magazine and it was very good and I was rather engrossed in it.'

'And can you tell me what Sylvia Hounslow and Mavis Turley were doing?'

'They were both reading I think. I can vaguely remember Sylvia mentioning some sort of collagen injection to stop wrinkles or something, but I can't quite remember. I'm sorry I sound rather vague.'

'Well if you can think of anything else, let us know!'

'I haven't been much help have I Inspector? But I've been so tired and under the weather lately. When I came her I didn't seem to notice much of what was going on . . . . I suppose it must have been the pregnancy. I feel great now though, full of beans.'

'I'm glad to hear it.' smiled the Inspector.

⁂ ⁂ ⁂

Peter was waiting for Celia when she came out. He questioned her discreetly but she assured him that the Inspector hadn't upset her. He felt very relieved.

'Come on darling, we'll go into town and see what's on at the theatre.'

'You seem in a good mood' she smiled.

'I'm just happy, I'm a lucky man having you, and the

baby on the way.'

✳ ✳ ✳

Tom knocked on the kitchen door.

'Don't get coming in here with those muddy boots on Tom, take them off and I'll get Mary to do you some tea.' Lil scowled.

'Is Mrs Richards about anywhere, I'd like a word with her.'

'I think she's too busy to be bothered with the garden now Tom.'

Just then George came in.

Alright Tom, tea break again eh.' he smiled.

'I was wondering if I could have a word with you?'

'Certainly,'

'In private?'

'Of course, come through.'

Mrs Burridge looked annoyed as they walked out of the kitchen. Mary smiled to herself 'I bet she's put out, she'll be wondering what's going on.'

'Done those dishes yet girl . . . . Get a move on' Lil snapped.

✳ ✳ ✳

'I was wondering sir, have you been doing any gardening lately?'

'Well I leave that to you Tom. You know I haven't had the time with all this business.'

'Only someone's opened my weedkiller and a fair amount has gone. It was a new bottle. I was keeping it for the weeds between the crazy paving.'

'Well it wasn't me Tom, I'll ask Rosemary later.'

✳ ✳ ✳

'Well I think it's rather odd' said Rosemary. 'I mean, a new bottle being opened. The Inspector was saying the other day about something possibly being put into the white wine sauce on the mussels to make Martha feel ill. You never know, it could have been the weedkiller!'

'Oh no, are you doing your amateur detective bit.'

'Make fun if you like, but I'm going to tell him.'

✳ ✳ ✳

Rosemary phoned the station the next day and gave the information to Roper. An hour or so later they arrived at the hotel to see Tom.

He explained that it was a new bottle that was sealed and that why he knew it had been opened.

'Do you leave the keys to the shed hanging anywhere Tom?' inquired Sergeant Roper.

'No, I always take them home with me. I've got that

shed just how I want it. Everythings in order.'

'We'll go and have a look then.'

The three of them went to the shed. It was a picture. All the tools were lined up and cleaned. The mower was sparkling. The canes were stacked neatly in the corner and all the fertilizers and chemicals stood beside each other with a pile of gardening books next to them.

'My word, I feel ashamed of my garden shed after looking at this' the Inspector said. Tom smiled proudly.

'This is why I take the keys home. Sometimes Mr Richards gets angry if he wants to get anything, but I don't like people poking around when I'm not here.'

'There's no window that could be forced open and the lock was not damaged. I can't see how anyone could have got in.' Roper sounded puzzled.

'Think Tom, are you sure you never left it open?'

'No sir, I'm sure of it. The only person who went in there was young Mr Bellamy.'

'Oh yes. What for?'

'He went in to borrow a gardening book. He seems very interested in gardening. I've got them all you know, Rose growing, hardy annuals, vegetables.:'

'Well you've been a great help Tom, thank you. I'll leave you to get on with your work.'

Just as they were leaving, they bumped into Rosemary,

'Any luck?'

'Well actually, the only person who had been in there was Peter Bellamy to borrow a book.'

'That's strange' said Rosemary.

'Why, isn't he keen on gardening?'

'Oh yes, he's always been interested. He potters about in the garden at home all the time Celia says. It's just that I bumped into him in our local library the other day and he said he was looking for gardening books, but I don't know why. Tom's got loads he could have borrowed. Anyway, must rush, I've got the accounts to do' she hurried away.

'Well I think we'll have to have another word with our Mr Bellamy, but first, I think we'll check his room.

✳ ✳ ✳

'I don't really like doing this' said George as he unlocked the door. He handed the keys to the Inspector and went to walk away.

'We'll be searching everyones room in time.' He assured him.

They both had a good look around and checked the drawers next to the bed.

'Doesn't seem to be anything here.'

As Roper was checking the pockets of a jacket hanging in the wardrobe he pulled out a bottle.

'Mogadon, sleeping tablets' said the Inspector.

'He doesn't seem the type to have sleepless nights unless he's spending them with a woman' sneered Roper.

'I think we'll have to have a word with him first thing

tomorrow.' They locked the room and left.

CHAPTER THIRTEEN

A tangled web

Roper was typing some reports.

'I wish I could have a better typewriter, perhaps an electronic one.'

'Be grateful for the one you've got lad, at least you're not writing them by hand.'

Inspector Trafford plugged his electric kettle in.

'We'll have a cup of tea it will be a nice change from that rubbish you drink down the canteen. Actually I'm quite looking forward to interviewing Mr. Bellamy, he seems to have a lot to hide.'

'Do you think we might have cracked it?' 'I doubt it' replied Inspector Trafford. 'Most people have things to hide. It may be nothing to do with the case, but these things have got to be cleared up. I think we'll obtain a warrant to search everyone's room.'

'I don't think they'll like that sir.'

'I'm not bothered whether they do or not!' he said stirring the tea.

'You can never find two socks that match.' George thought to himself. He was getting really angry. 'Rosemary never sorts the washing out. I bet she's got my socks in her underwear drawer.' He opened it and was sorting through, when he came across the Building Society books, it was in joint names. 'Always keeps the book she does, must be worried I'll draw some money out and have a bet' he mused to himself.

He opened it up and looked at the balance. It was considerably less than he'd expected. 'That's funny, she normally was so careful with money' he thought. He carried on going through the book and noticed that withdrawals of one hundred and fifty pounds were being taken out every month on the same day. What the hells this' he thought 'I'll have to have a word with Rosemary.'

* * *

'What is it now Inspector?' Peter Bellamy looked angry and apprehensive at the same time.

'Look Mr. Bellamy, if you don't want your wife upset and us to keep calling upon you, I suggest that you answer our questions.'

'I've told you all I know.'

'Is it true,' inquired Inspector Trafford 'that you have a relationship with Mrs Sylvia Hounslow?'

'Rubbish!'

'I also put it to you that a bottle of weedkiller is missing from Tom's shed. He tells me you've been in there a lot lately.'

'Only to get gardening books.I've touched nothing else.

'Do you have trouble sleeping Mr Bellamy? Any conscious problems?' Roper added.

'I sleep like a log.'

What's this then?' Inspector Trafford slammed a bottle of Mogadon on the table.

'Where did you get that? How dare you go into my room.'

'Well if that's not yours, I'm sure your wife couldn't be taking them. She's a sensible woman. she knows that any tablets can harm the child in the first few months of pregnancy.'

Peter eyes started to fill up as he desperately tried to control his feelings.

'I've done something terrible' he said. 'Will she ever forgive me?'

Roper thought he was going to confess to the murder, but Inspector Trafford had different ideas.

Peter straightened himself up and seemed to take control.

'If I tell you everything Inspector, do you promise that what I've said will never reach my wife's ears?'

'Unless it's relevant to the case, I won't say anything. We're not here to cause trouble in anyone's marriage, we just want to find Martha Hounslow's murderer.'

'I've always been a bit of a womaniser, although I do love my wife. I've had a bit of an on off affair with Sylvia.

She's got plenty of money but she's bored with her marriage like most women. I think I was a bit of excitement for her.

Martha seemed to cotton on that there was something going on between us and threatened to tell Celia. I didn't think she would, but then you never can tell?'

'So she didn't want her son hurt?' asked Roper.

'Well actually, I don't think it was that. I think she'd have been glad to see the back of Sylvia, but thought a divorce would be bad for William's business.'

'So you cooled it?'

'Well yes . . .But not because of that, I'd have finished it anyway what with the baby coming.'

'But you did say you'd like to kill her didn't you Mr. Bellamy?'

'Well yes but only in temper. I wouldn't risk being banged up for her.'

'Yes, but you'd have risked your marriage?'

'Quite frankly, I don't think she'd have done anything about it. I think she was just trying to frighten me.'

'And what about these?' Inspector Trafford held up the bottle. His face changed dramatically.

'I think I may have committed a murder, but not the one you're thinking of Inspector. . . ' he started to explain . . .

'So you say you gave the Mogadon to your wife to make sure she stayed asleep.' said Inspector Trafford.

'Yes, that's right, it sounds awful doesn't it just for

sex and that's all it was so she wouldn't wake and find me missing.'

'And what about Mr Hounslow, did Sylvia give him any?'

'Well according to Sylvia, William used to sleep like a log, so he'd never know she was missing.'

'I see' said Roper 'and where would you go?'

He was really enjoying this, it had the thrill of a porn movie.

'Oh one of the bathrooms, or landings.'

'A bit uncomfortable on the hard floor eh?' Roper sneered.

Inspector Trafford became very annoyed, 'That'll be enough Sergeant.'

'You see Inspector, I didn't realise then that Celia was pregnant. Of course I know you're not supposed to take any tablets in the early stages of pregnancy as they can affect the baby. I feel so bad about it.'

'Well perhaps you ought to go and see a doctor and tell him how much you've given her, and perhaps tell your wife.'

'I couldn't do that Inspector.'

'Can you tell me, do you know anything about some missing weedkiller out of Tom's shed?'

'Oh my God, you don't think I'd give my wife that? I feel bad enough about Mogadon?'

'Well I believe you were in there getting a gardening book?'

'Yes, that's right.'

'So why were you getting a gardening book from the library as well?

"Actually, I wasn't. I was in the medical section trying to find books on pregnancy to see what effects these Mogadon tablets would have on Celia and the baby."

"Well that sound quite plausible. I think that will be all for now."

Peter turned at the door and went to speak.

"Don't worry, we won't say anything to your wife at this stage but I suggest you get medical advice."

"I will. I definitely will" he assured them.

After he had gone Roper turned to the Inspector 'Well what do you think?"

"I believe him."

'So do I . . . I suppose' He sounded unsure.

"He'd gain nothing financially from her death just peace of mind about his wife not finding out about his affair with Sylvia Hounslow."

" But he could always deny it."

"Well, before he was just a married man having a bit on the side, but now he's going to be a father, maybe he's more responsible and yet a leopard never changes his spots. Oh well let's carry on searching the rooms and see what we can find."

Sylvia Hounslow's is next on the list I think."

✳ ✳ ✳

They'd been in the room for about twenty minutes.

"Nothing much here." said Roper "But my wife would kill for some of these dresses."

"Clothes do not make a woman, Roper."

"You don't think so eh?" smiled Roper.

Inspector Trafford was sifting through the dressing table. Nail varnishes in so many colours with matching lipsticks were all lined up.

'My God when my wife was younger, there was only red to choose from. Now that's funny' he picked up a nail file with red along the edge.

"Get this taken to the lab Roper."

Roper put it in a polythene bag.

"What for?"

"Never mind what for, just do it."

* * *

They all sat round the lounge with after dinner coffee. William walked in from using the phone.

"I'm bloody fed up with all this. I want to get mother's body back and start the funeral arrangements. I've been onto the office, there's a problem with a big order, I could have done with getting back home."

"Well I'd like Celia to go back and see our doctor with the baby and everything."

"I'm alright Darling. Rosemary's doctor is keeping an eye on me."

"I don't know what all the fuss is about. I'm getting a good rest, plenty of fishing" Simon said with an air of contentment.

"Well I need to get back and start up my market stall" said Dave. "I'm really short of cash at the moment."

"Well I could lend you some' said William.

"Well that's awfully nice of you . . . ."

"No, Dave wouldn't hear of it, would you?" Rosemary interrupted.

"Er . . . . no . . . . . It's alright old chap, thanks a lot anyway. I've got a couple of cards up my sleeve. I know where there's a bit of a deal in the offing."

"What's that?" asked Celia.

"Can't really say" Dave smirked. "But let's just say I've got some information that might be useful."

"Oh Dave, you and your deals." George laughed.

"Well I'm don't know about your business Dave, but all this publicity won't be any good for ours." said Rosemary depressingly.

"Oh I don't know" said Peter "It'll all blow over, you've both worked hard, you've got a nice place here. You'll be okay."

"That's what I've told her" said George. "and we're thinking of doing some special Christmas breaks, getting an entertainer in, a three day special, you know the sort of thing."

"Sounds good" said Dave "Now I know a D.J. . . . . ."

They all laughed and changed the subject leaving Dave looking dejected.

CHAPTER FOURTEEN

The Scarlet Lady

Inspector Trafford sat at his desk staring out of the window. He felt old and tired. I suppose most people wouldn't class late fifties as ancient, just well into middle age. His mother still thought of him as a youngster, and fussed over him, but with all these young men coming into the force he felt decidely past it.

'Even Roper says I'm an old stick-in-the-mud' he mused.

He'd been with the West Country Police a good many years and had solved his fair share of cases since his transfer to the murder squad eight years ago. He wasn't keen on using these Hi-tech computers like Roper and the rest of the lads, preferring to rely on his own intuition in cases like these, but he thought this one was proving too difficult and maybe he was losing his touch.

His thoughts turned to Martha Hounslow. She had still maintained a lot of spirit even at seventy according to the others and the gusto and determination of a much younger woman, maybe that trait in her could have led to her death. Perhaps someone wasn't prepared to put up with her bullying, and yet murder? Was it the same old thing most people murder for – money. He'd have to go through the lists of guests again, was there something, somewhere he had missed.

'I am getting old' he thought.

Just at that moment Sergeant Roper came in. 'This letters just arrived from Martha Hounslow's solicitors.'

'Oh yes, I requested details of her last Will and Testament.' He opened the letter and read it carefully.

'Much as we thought, the only person to benefit really is her son. He gets her house plus all the money, investments, stocks and shares etc. She left a thousand pounds and a couple of pictures to her sister and that's about it.'

'Maybe they're very valuable pictures and they're worth thousands.' mused Roper 'And her sister's here incognito and murdered her.'

'I'm sure if the pictures were valuable, Martha Hounslow would have known. No Roper, if money was the motive it's got to be William or Sylvia.'

'And yet he said she wasn't going to get her hands on the money.'

'Well she's entitled to quite a sum if they divorce'.

'I should imagine that she'd buy a seductive nightie and offer him a night of lurid passion. He'd be putty in her hands and she'd have anything she wanted.'

'I doubt that Roper, you young men think that sex is

the be-all and end-all of everything. Maybe in his younger days he would have succumbed, but I think he's a lot wiser now.'

Just at that moment the phone rang.

'It's the lab Sir, they want to speak to you.'

Inspector Trafford reached for the phone.

'Car paint you say, mmm just as I thought, thanks a lot.' He put the phone down and smiled to himself. Maybe it wasn't going to be such a bad day after all.

※ ※ ※

Sylvia Hounslow walked into the room. She was wearing a red trouser suit that was beautifully tailored although a little tight and just enough gold jewellery to enhance it.

'Good morning Inspector, I gather you want to speak to me?'

'Yes. Please take a seat Mrs Hounslow.'

'I've told you Sylvia, haven't I?' She sat down. 'I see you don't have that nice young Sergeant with you today?' she smiled.

'No, he's got a lot of paperwork.'

'Mmm . . . . pity' she lit a cigarette.

'Do you recognise this?' Inspector Trafford placed a nail file on the table which had which had a red mark along one edge.

'Well it's a nail file. I don't know whether it's mine or not, I've got several.'

'Well it was found in your bedroom!'

'Well then I suppose it must be. I can't see the point Inspector.'

'Well we've had it analysed. This isn't nail polish along the edge, it's red car paint off your husband's car.'

'Really, you amaze me Inspector' She blew smoke into the air. 'Mind you, looking at it, it's not the colour of the nail polish I use, mine all match my lipsticks.'

'Yes I noticed that myself.'

'Well how observant of you Inspector, I wouldn't have thought you'd have known about things like that?'

'You know what this implies don't you?'

'What . . . . you think I scratched William's precious car with it?'

'Well its a possibility.'

'I know I can be a bitch Inspector, but I wouldn't stoop as low as that.'

'Maybe it was for a specific reason.'

'What do you mean?'

'Well it was when all the men were outside looking at the car that I believe the weed killer was put into Martha Hounslow's starter in order to make her ill.'

'Oh I see. So you think I scratched the car on purpose to get them all out there. Well I would have got rid of the nail file wouldn't I?'

'Not necessarily, you might not have thought you needed to.'

'Well William could have scratched the car himself.'

'I believe that car is is his pride and joy. You really think he would do that?'

'Why not? He could always get it resprayed. He'll have enough money to buy ten Jaguars now anyway. Look Inspector, it wasn't me. Maybe someone else used the file and put it back in my room.'

'Has anyone been in there lately?'

'No I don't think so, only Mary the cleaner.'

'Well that's all for now Mrs Hounslow.'

'Am I a suspect now Inspector?'

'You're all suspects . . . .'

'But maybe I'm the prime suspect' She said dryly as she left.

After she had gone, Inspector Trafford thought to himself 'She doesn't seem to be taking this seriously . . . She wasn't perturbed when I showed her the nail file . . . either she really doesn't know anything about it or she's an excellent actress.'

* * *

Inspector Trafford was discussing Sylvia Hounslow's interview with Roper.

'So she asked about me did she?' he beamed.

'Alright Roper, so your male ego has been boosted – let's keep to the facts shall we?'

'Well it seems to me that the nail file was used by someone in the house to scratch the car, even if it wasn't Mrs Hounslow.'

'Precisely' agreed Inspector Trafford 'I didn't think

for a minute it was teenage vandals.'

'I suppose it is possible for someone to have taken it off Mrs Hounslow's dressing table, used it to scratch the car and replaced it.'

'Quite possible.'

'Well sir, whoever it is, they must have known if the file was found it would incriminate Mrs Hounslow.'

'Precisely . . . . it's someone who doesn't like her.'

'I should think' said Roper, 'They'd hate her if they wanted her accused of murder.'

'Well perhaps they just wanted to mislead us. Since there have been no attempts on William Hounslow's life, I think we can take it that Martha Hounslow was the intended victim. The Dixogin was specifically put into her medicine and although all William's mussels weren't eaten, I think we can assume the weedkiller was in the white wine sauce.'

'But what if for some reason Martha hadn't taken the stomach medicine?'

'Well then I suppose the murderer would have had to try something else.'

'Do you think we can exclude Mr & Mrs Richards from our list of suspects?'

'No we can't. They asked her down here. There could have been a motive.William and Sylvia Hounslow are still pretty high on the list and I'm still not dismissing Peter Bellamy. His story sounds plausible, but I still think he's keeping something from us.'

'Well surely his wife isn't involved?'

'We don't know that either' said Inpector Trafford 'She seems to worship her husband, if Martha Hounslow had said anything about him to enrage her, who knows?'

'Mmm, you could be right there. They say a woman's hormones go haywire in pregnancy, funny mood swings. I remember my wife was touchy. Then there's Mavis and Simon Turley. He seems innocent enough and she's just a carpet for him to walk all over.'

'Well, maybe he resents anyone with money. He says it doesn't bother him, but it might do and down trodden women have been known to turn.'

'And what about Flash Harry?' laughed Roper.

'Our dear Mr Cranmore. Wheeled and dealed all his life, possible. She could have known something about a shady deal, threatened to expose him. Still a possibility there, no Roper, we can't exclude anyone yet, not even the staff. God we've got that much to do, my brain needs shaking up, I don't know where to start. I'm going home now. I think I'll try and get an hour in the garden, it might help clear my head.'

'Okay sir, see you tomorrow.'

※ ※ ※

William and Mavis walked along the beach hand in hand.

'You've been a God send Mavis. I'd have never got through this without you, and you mean what you say about coming away with me, you won't change your mind?'

'No I mean it William. Simon can get on alright without me and he'll have to stand on his own two feet sometime.'

'Well there's plenty of money now, I mean you can let Simon have the house if you want.'

'Well I've worked hard and contributed a lot towards it. I bought most of the furniture.'

'Well, we'll have all our own. Mavis, we'll start afresh. There's plenty of money, we'll go on a cruise and look for somewhere when we get back.'

'Oh William it sounds wonderful, but what about your business?'

'It'll survive without me. I've got a good management team, they can run things while I'm away.'

Mavis suddenly stopped and turned. The sea breeze blowing her hair into her eyes, she pushed it away.

'And what about Sylvia?'

'She'll be okay. I'll provide for her and she can go off with whoever she likes. Mother had an old fashioned attitude. Nowadays divorce doesn't make much difference. Most of my business associates never really liked or respected Sylvia. They may have fancied her for a quick lay.'

'And do you fancy me for a quick lay?' She grabbed hold of William teasingly.

'I need you Mavis.'

'Well what more could a woman ask for?' she smiled.

He pulled her towards him and smothered her face

with kisses.

'I know you're heart broken over your mother William. I feel bad because you're so sad, but I'll be a mother, lover, mistress, wife, everything to you.'

'I know you will Mavis.'

They continued walking . . . .

'I suppose you wouldn't have been so financially secure as you are now if your mother had still been alive?'

'We'd have managed Mavis, I've never been short.'

'But money's nothing anyway. It's love that really counts isn't it William?'

'Yes, but I've seen lots of marriages break up because of money problems Mavis. It does count.'

She moved away from him and studied him carefully. He caught that look in her eye.

'Was it a look of distrust' he thought.

'Mavis, you don't think that I'd got anything to do with Mother's death do you? I mean you couldn't love a man who'd done that, I mean no woman could!'

'Oh I suppose a certain type of woman could, but I don't think that darling. I saw the sorrow in your eyes, I knew it was genuine' she thought to herself as she looked out to sea.

'Yes it was the same look of sorrow he had in the church that day at Cockington. This man could never murder anybody, this was the man she loved wasn't it? Oh I do love him. I must get these thoughts out of my head.'

CHAPTER FIFTEEN

'Exit the Joker'

It was a Monday afternoon. The day had been warm and hazy, the sea looked like dark blue glass. Inspector Trafford's office was hot and stuffy even with the windows open. He decided he had had enough for one day and went home early to do some gardening.

He loved his garden, it was his haven when life got complicated.

He'd been busy planting flowers and trimming the borders and felt hot and sticky so he decided to take a well earned rest. He sat back on the bench drinking an ice cold beer and admiring his work. The phone in the hall rang.

Mrs Trafford wiped her hands on her apron.

'Who's that now?' she thought 'I don't want my Yorkshires to go flat.' She answered the phone.

'Oh yes alright, I'll get him if it's really necessary.'

She opened the lounge window and called to her husband. 'John, the stations on the phone.'

Inspector Trafford walked in with his beer. 'No peace for the wicked. That beef smells nice, shall I open some red wine?'

'I wouldn't count on your dinner dear' She handed him the phone.

He listened for a few minutes.

'I can't see why they've called us. Don't they know we're investigating a murder? We've got enough to do' he sounded angry.

'Well sir, PC Lewis who came to the Richard's house with us one day is at the scene and he thinks that the body looks like Mr Cranmore's. He can't be sure of course because the face is disfigured, but he thought you ought to know before they remove the body.'

Oh yes . . . quite so Roper. I'll be there directly.

Mrs Trafford was slicing the beef and the smell waffed through into the hallway.

'Mmm . . . pity about the dinner' The Inspector sniffed

'You sound like a Bisto kid, John. Don't worry, I'll keep it warm.'

'Don't bother I may be a long time.'

✳ ✳ ✳

It was still sunny even though it was late afternoon. The sea at Babbacombe looked calm. 'It's funny how nature stays the same he thought as he looked around. A life cut short and everything looks so peaceful.

The Forensic and the photographer were there with Sergeant Roper and PC Lewis. They were cordoning off the area. Inspector Trafford could see for himself the body was that of Dave Cranmore.

'You did well to spot him son. He turned to PC Lewis who gave a quick smile.

'Thank you sir' Inspector Trafford walked down to Tom Purvis the Police Doctor who was bending over the body. He stood up and shook his hand.

'How are you John?'

'I've had better days' he grunted. 'Is there anything you can tell me?'

'Well I think he had been drinking. Difficult to say the amount he consumed till we get the pathologist's report. From what I can tell his injuries tie up with the fall. There are several head wounds and broken bones, at a guess I'd say the cause of death was probably the skull being crushed on impact with the rocks.'

'Could he have been hit on the head and pushed over?'

'Quite possible the head injuries could have been caused by blows. He could have been unconscious before he fell. I gather he was involved in a murder inquiry?'

'Well he was a suspect along with several others. Still we've one suspect less now.' Roper remarked.

'Yes but we could have another murder to solve.' the Inspector sounded depressed.

'Well this is all speculation, lets see what the coroner's report say.' the police doctor sounded positive.

'Thanks for your help Tom. I'll be in touch' the Inspector nodded.

Just before he moved way. He looked down at the body. The clothes and shoes looked cheap and worn. Inspector Trafford suddenly felt very sorry for the deceased.

'He'd probably never had much.' he thought. 'Always trying to strike up a deal. Never finding that lucky break that could make him a fortune.'

They walked back up to the top. Dave's old 'V' reg car was parked on the road.

'Probably never had an M.O.T. on the car. It looks a death trap.' Sergeant Roper remarked. 'What do you think you Sir? I mean it's a bit of a coincidence, could he have just fallen? He'd had a drink he could have missed his footing. He did a lot of wheeling and dealing maybe his past caught up with him.'

'I doubt if he was in with any dangerous villians, or drugs. I think he was just small time, poor little sod.' The Inspector replied.

'Shall I let them know at the hotel?'

'Yes I think you'd better Roper although someone may know already.'

'You mean he was bumped off by one of them?'

'Quite possible, he could have known something or was blackmailing one of them. I'll stay here and look around for a while I'll see you later.

The seafront at Babbacombe was quite high. It had railings all along until you reached the left hand side were the lift ran down to the beach. If you didn't want to get a lift down you could walk or drive down a steep winding road but where Dave had gone over at the far end it was a much steeper drop to the sea and there were lots of trees and bushes all the way down.

It was an ideal place to push some-one over, and yet perhaps he may have been able to save himself and break his fall by trying to grab hold of one of the bushes or shrubs.

'I'll get the car checked out and then have word with forensic and then tomorrow its back to the Sherwell Hotel!' he thought.

CHAPTER SIXTEEN

The alibis

'All the women were crying, even Sylvia.

'I can't believe it' said Rosemary 'I told him not to drink.'

'Well we don't know he was drunk yet?' remarked George.

'Oh he probably was, he'd had a few before he went out' said Simon.

'Well maybe someone from his seedy past caught up with him.' said Peter. 'He'd done a few dirty deals you know.'

'Yes, but they'd never follow him all the way down here would they?' asked Mavis.

'Why not? It all depends what he's done.'

'I can't believe this, I don't want to stay here anymore. I don't feel safe, what about my baby?' Celia started to sob.

'Maybe none of us are safe?' said Sylvia.

'What do you mean?' William asked.

'Well first Martha, now Dave, what most of you haven't thought is, he could have been murdered.'

'I think that's a bit far fetched' said Simon. 'You women are so melodramatic.'

'Well I suppose that Inspector chap and his Sergeant will be snooping around again.' Peter sounded depressed.

'There's a curse on this hotel. We should never have bought it. It's like a nightmare.' Rosemary ran out of the room.

* * *

Inspector Trafford and Roper were in the office.

'So let's just recap' said Inspector Trafford. Roper started reading from his note pad.

'PC Lewis found him at approximately midday on Monday and the coroner reckons he'd been dead for about fifteen to sixteen hours. That would make the time of death approximately eight to nine pm on Sunday night.'

'Mmm' Inspector Trafford scratched his head. 'He could have fallen or been pushed down earlier, say at seven o'clock and probably took an hour or two to die.'

'Do you think he was conscious, sir?'

'I doubt it from the head injuries. The Coroner said he would have had severe concussion and been in a coma. I don't think he ever regained conciousness. Probably a good job really.'

'So we'll have to get alibis and statements from them. All that rigmarole again, I mean it could just have been an accident, 'he sounded despondent.

'Yes, that's always a possibility, but it's too much of a coincidence in my opinion. I've spoken to the coroner, he said it's possible that he was hit over the head or the injuries could have been due to the impact on hitting the rocks. He'd been drinking, but not a tremendous amount. On the way down, there were lots of bushes. I would have thought he could have perhaps grabbed one to try to save himself, but if he was knocked on the head and then pushed over, he would have been unconscious as he went down.'

'Are we looking for a man then. I mean surely it would require a certain amount of strength?'

'Well if he was hit on the head and dazed or say he felt giddy, it would be quite easy for a woman to push him over!'

'Do you think they went to see if he was dead?'

'That's very doubtful, they could have fallen themselves. No I think if he was pushed, the murderer would get away as soon as possible.'

'But how about if he'd survived and could identify the person who'd pushed him?'

'Well that's unlikely but it was a chance the murderer would have to take. Actually Roper, if Dave was murdered it must have been the same person that murdered Martha Hounslow. They took a chance then that only one person would take the stomach medicine and they've taken another chance now.'

'Does that mean that they like to gamble, Russian Roulette and all that eh?' Roper said lightly.

'That or they're desperate. Oh God, so am I. There's something I've missed somewhere, Roper . . . . . . something I've missed!'

* * *

The Inspector drove towards the Sherwell Hotel.

'I was thinking sir, wouldn't the guests all have an alibi. I mean they'd have been at the evening meal wouldn't they and Mr and Mrs Richards would have been helping to serve it?'

'Monday to Saturday yes. But they do a Sunday lunch instead of an evening meal like most hotels' Inspector Trafford replied.

'So any other night but Sunday they'd have all been there.'

Precisely, so you see that's too much of a coincidence.'

* * *

When they arrived the Inspector explained to Rosemary and George that they would have to check on the whereabouts of everyone at the time that Dave had died.

Rosemary went to get those that were in while

George saw Inspector Trafford and Sergeant Roper went into the study.

'May I ask where you were on Sunday evening sir?'

'Actually Inspector, I was stuck here doing the books and accounts. It's normally Rosemary's job, she won't let me touch them, usually, but lately she hasn't been bothered. She went to see a friend. I thought it would do her good. She's been very upset with the strain of it all. We both liked Dave you know Inspector, for all his faults.'

'Those are the best friends' said the Inspector. 'The ones who still like us with all our faults and weaknesses.'

Rosemary came in.

'A few of them are here Inspector, who do you want to see first?'

'Whoever's there. By the way, I believe you visited a friend on Sunday evening?'

'Oh yes, Janet Morgan, she lives just this side of the River Dart. It did me good to get out.'

'And what time did you leave?'

'Oh about six thirty and I was back at about ten thirty or thereabouts. I think, I'd left George doing the accounts so I thought I'd better do him a bit of supper. But when I got back he'd gone out with Simon.'

'Right thanks a lot, that will be all for now.'

Roper showed Celia in. They inquired about her health and she said she felt fine. She was upset by it all but said she was too busy concentrating on her own well being for the sake of the baby, which Roper and the Inspector commended. Celia explained she was in bed at eight as she was rather tired and she'd slept through until the next morning.

❋ ❋ ❋

When Peter came in he sounded rather vague.

'I just potted about the hotel actually Inspector. Celia had an early night and I felt at a loose end. I had a couple of games of pool by myself and strolled down to the park as it was a fine evening.'

'Did you see anyone?'

'To tell you the truth, I didn't, ... Oh I saw George in the office when I left, but he looked busy so I never distubed him.'

'I actually believe that' thought Inspector Trafford. 'He didn't really quite know what he was doing or what time it was and yet it sounded genuine.'

❋ ❋ ❋

When Simon came in, Roper glanced at Inspector Trafford. 'I think I'll keep this as brief as possible' he thought.

'Bad show eh Inspector? Bit of a lad you know our Dave. Could have been bumped off, could have been drunk as a lord, who knows? Never had much in his life you know. I told him, get back to nature that's what it's all about, now look at me!'

'We really must get on Sir. Now your whereabouts on the night in question?'

'Oh yes Inspector. Well poor George stuck in the office doing the books, Rosemary's job by all accounts . . . .' he suddenly laughed realising his joke.'Well I made him come into town for a drink. I think we left at about 8 o'clock. Never got back till late.'

'But listen. I never told you this before because I didn't think it was worth mentioning. But now Dave's been pushed off a cliff . . . I mean you can't be too careful can you?'

'We we don't know for certain, but we think there may have been foul play.' Roper interrupted.

'Well one day at Dartmouth we all took a trip down the river and some-one pushed me off the boat!'

'Did you see who it was?' asked the Inspector.

'Of course not, I'd have bloody killed him!'

'It could have been a woman' suggested Roper.

'A woman couldn't push me over.'

'Well no-one's mentioned this before.' the Inspector sounded suspicious.

'That's because they all think, I was drunk and lost my footing. No one believed me. Now I think whoever murdered Dave is trying to kill me.

'Can you think of any reason why anyone should want you dead Mr Turley?'

'None whatsoever. I'm a genial sort of chap liked by

148

everyone.'

'I doubt that' thought Trafford.

'And another thing Dave never came with us the day we went to Dartmouth. So you see he couldn't have pushed me. Well he's gone now anyway.'

'We'll look into this then Mr Turley.'

'Don't you think I need police protection?'

'Not at this stage. It will have to be investigated though.'

'Just make sure you do Inspector.'

'Well thanks a lot Mr Turley. Is your wife about?'

'She's not here at the moment but she should be back later.'

'What do you think of that then Roper?'

'I don't know, I mean, he's always drinking. I suppose he could have fallen, he's a bit melodramatic. Maybe he was driving everyone mad about his fishing and they pushed him over as a joke.'

'That's quite possible, but it's odd isn't it? . . . . Martha Hounslow, Dave Cranmore . . . . could he be victim number three I wonder?'

✳ ✳ ✳

Sylvia was the next one to be interviewed. She was her normal friendly self and tried to flirt with Roper which he enjoyed immensely.

She told the inspector that on Sunday night she had stayed in to do her beauty routine. Face pack, nails, deep condition her hair.

'And did you see anyone?'

'No, it was quiet in the hotel. Oh no, I tell a lie, Mavis popped in for a few moments to return a peach lipstick I'd lent her some time ago.'

'And what time was that do you know?'

'Well I was in the bath when she came in and I asked her the time as I was timing the conditioner on my hair. If you leave it on too long your hair goes too lank and greasy, and I think she said it was about seven fifteen.'

Sylvia didn't seem to be able to give them anymore information.

'I don't see that any of them have got good alibis.' said Roper. 'They all seem to be alone. Sylvia doing her beauty routine. Peter out walking, Celia in bed, anyone of them could be lying. I suppose George and Simon's alibis are okay?'

'Not necessarily' Inspector Trafford straightened his bow tie. Peter says he saw George go for a drink at eight, what was he doing before then? Rosemary has an alibi if the time checks out with her friend. Get onto that will you Roper?'

'Okay sir.'

'Now let's see who haven't we seen. Just William Hounslow, Mavis Turley and the staff. I think we'll see Mr Hounslow next.' William came in looking rather concerned and shaken.

'Do you think it's connected anyway to Mother's death. I mean you don't know for sure Dave was murdered do you?'

'Well not yet but it's a possibility, two deaths in such a short time, too much of a coincidence don't you think?'

'Well I've racked my brains since our last meeting Inspector and I still can't think of any reason why anyone should kill my mother. Now Dave . . . . is a different kettle of fish. He's done a lot of bad deals, so it's possible he'd trod on someone's toes and I think he was short of money. In fact I even offered to lend him some the other night. I must be getting soft in my old age. but do you know, he refused said he'd got some information, some deal going.'

'Really. That sounds interesting. He didn't say what it was by any chance?'

'No, not Dave, he just wanted us to know about it.'

'Now Sir, we believe Mr Cranmore was killed at between seven forty-five and nine fifteen on Sunday evening. Could you tell us of your whereabouts?'

'Well I was with Mavis . . . er . . . Mrs Turley. We went for a walk and then had a few drinks in town and then we went for a meal as there was no evening meal at the hotel.'

'Really, and what about Mr Turley, didn't he mind?'

'He's got a gem there, and he doesn't appreciate her. He'd have only gone out drinking and left her in.'

'And your wife?'

'There's no love lost between my wife and I Inspector. We are together now for convenience sake. I believe it was her beauty night or something. If I'd have stopped in she'd have been hours in the bathroom. I'd never have seen her anyway.'

'Is there something more than just friendship between you and Mrs Turley?' Roper inquired.

'How dare you insinuate such a thing' He went red in the face. 'She's a lovely woman, she's got a heart of gold. I feel sorry for her that's all, if I can give her a little happiness why not? She's never really had much it's a shame. I mean when I met her you should have seen the poor old lace-up shoes she'd got on. Sylvia's got about twenty pairs of shoes, one for each outfit. No, she deserves better . . . a lot better than him.'

'Now can tell me what time you met Mrs Turley?'

'Well I'm not sure, I'd mislaid my watch, but I think it was about seven thirty or thereabouts.'

'And you spent the whole evening together?'

'Yes, I think we got back about ten thirty.'

'Well thank you Mr Hounslow, that will be all for now.'

※ ※ ※

After he'd gone Roper turned to Inspector Trafford. 'He seems a lot happier doesn't he? He appears to have got over his mother. He even wanted to chat about Mr Cranmore who he normally considered to be a waster.'

'When people are in love they become more genial. They have more patience and understanding with their fellow beings.'

'So you don't believe that bit about him and Mrs Turley being just good friends?'

'Do you?' Inspector Trafford asked.

✳ ✳ ✳

As Mrs Turley was unavailable to be interviewed, Inspector Trafford decided to speak to Mrs Burridge.

She had been at home with her husband and daughter. Sunday night was her night off and her daughter normally came round for 'a bit of tea' as she put it.

She had spoken to Mr Cranmore earlier that morning as he was always popping into the kitchen and pinching a slice of cake or anything that was going and he seemed in a really good mood, almost excited about something.

Mary was at home with her parents on Sunday night, but she did mention Mr Cranmore teasing her in the kitchen the day before saying he would take her away from all this when he had money.

Lil had sent him packing as Mary had work to do.

Just as William was turning the corner of Sherwell Hill he bumped into Mavis.

'Hello darling, that Inspector chap wants a word with you about Sunday night. I told him we were together all evening so there's nothing to worry about.'

He suddenly went a little red and quiet.

'What's the matter?' Mavis asked.

'Well, he asked me about our relationship. I was tempted to tell him. But I thought I'd better make out we were just friends, not that it makes any difference, but you never know.'

'That's Okay, I understand' she assured him.

'Look Mavis, I don't care who knows about us. I'll tell Sylvia and Simon anytime you like. It's just that I thought with Dave's death and all that . . .'

She put her arms around his neck and kissed him.

'I know you would darling. I must dash if he's waiting to see me' and she walked away from him up the hill.

✳ ✳ ✳

When Mavis entered the room she looked quite smart. She had a blue shift dress on and a nice pair of blue shoes.

'She looks okay to me, doesn't look that much like a rag doll' thought Roper to himself.

'Now Mrs Turley, as you know, we are trying to determine the whereabouts of people on the evening of Mr Cranmore's death.'

Mavis looked sad.

'He was nice you know, Dave, a bit of a lad but nice.'

'So you can't think of anyone who want him dead?'

'Only the tax man perhaps.' and she smiled. Then she looked almost guilty that she'd cracked a joke under these solemn circumstances.

She confirmed that she'd met William about seven fifteen to seven thirty and they'd spent the whole evening together.

'Are you sure of the time, only Mr Hounslow hadn't got his watch on?

'I know, a lovely gold one and he'd mislaid it somewhere. Careless of him. Yes I had my watch on, it keeps excellent time.' She rolled her cuff back and showed them a neat little Timex. 'Did you have a nice evening?' Roper intervened.

'Yes lovely, he's a very kind man, William. Sylvia was having a night in and he knew Simon would be out drinking with someone. We were both at a loose end so we arranged to meet. We walked along the Meadfoot beach and up the cliffs then into town and had a meal in The Queens, a lovely little restaurant by the harbour, do you know it?'

'Yes it serves good food. a bit pricey for me though.' Roper smiled.

'You don't think Mrs Hounslow minded?' asked Inspector Trafford.

'Why she should mind about me? I'm not exactly the glamourous type.'

'You're a fine looking woman Mrs Turley and don't let anyone tell you otherwise' the Inspector said encouragingly.

Mavis lowered her lids and blushed.

'You've made her day' Roper remarked as she went out.'

Before they left the Inspector went to see Rosemary and George. He told them of his conversation with Simon.

'I haven't asked the others yet about him supposedly being pushed in the river . . . what's your opinion?'

'Well I was on the top deck with Mavis when he went over and we went running down. I must admit we all thought it was an accident. He'd had so much to drink. He was unsteady on his feet and there was a lot of schoolchildren running about.'

'At the time I completely dismissed the incident of him being pushed as did everyone else. But when it was confirmed that Martha was murdered I became anxious and I went to see Andy, a friend of ours who owns the boat. Apparently he's seen it all from his little cabin at. Some schoolchildren were rushing about and one of them knocked him and with all he'd had to drink he just toppled over.'

'Can we contact this man to get a statement?' asked the Inspector.

'Yes I've got his card somewhere.' George left the room for a few minutes.

When he returned he handed the Inspector a card which read. 'Mr Andrew Withers' 'Dart Cruises'

It had the appropriate address and telephone number on.

'Thanks a lot.' said the Inspector. They said their goodbyes and departed.

They were just driving off when Sergeant Roper

turned to the Inspector ' Do you think the story will check out?'

'I don't see why not . . . you can go and speak to him Roper . . . I'm quite relieved in a way. I mean if someone was trying to murder Simon Turley that would make this even more complicated. The trouble is with someone like that, who exaggerates all the time. People don't believe then when they are telling the truth.'

'Like the boy who cried wolf?'

"Precisely!' Trafford replied.

A mobile unit and been set up on Babbacombe Downs from which enquiries were now taking place.

The following day Inspector Trafford received a call from the forensic department to say they'd got some results for him. They were greeted by a Mr. Richard Littlejohn, one of the forensic scientists and an old friend of Inspector Traffords.

'How are you John?'

He shook his hand warmly.

'I've got a bit of useful information for you. To start with after an extensive examination of the victims head injuries, we find they are not all consistent with the fall.

'In what way?'.

'Well there's an injury to the top of the head which I believe was due to a blow and the indent in the skull seems to indicate it was probably done with something like a hammer or some similar instrument.'

'Do you think he was dead before he went over the cliff?'

'I don't think he was dead, just unconscious. He may have survived the blow to the head, he may have had brain damage, there's no way of determining that really.'

'At last light at the end of the tunnel' the Inspector smiled jubilantly. 'So we've got a weapon to look for?'

'Well the best is yet to come.' Mr Littlejohn said rather proudly. 'We found particles of nylon under the fingernails on the victims right hand. We've done test on the particles and they're the same substance used in women's tights and stockings, we've excelled ourselves this time John, we've tested tights on the market and they're the cheaper brand.'

'I thought all tights were the same price?' inquired the Inspector.

'You can pay up to five pounds for a decent pair, my wife pays about fifty pence a pair from the local market. I think most woman don't pay much more.'

'Trust you to know about that Roper.'

'Well you know I'm a leg man Sir' he laughed. 'When I was going through Sylvia Hounslow's room, I noticed all her tights were the expensive sort. I would say Mrs. Turley and Mrs Richards would buy cheap tights. Mrs Turley because she's got no money to spend on herself and Mrs Richards because she's too practical and wouldn't dream of buying expensive tights working all day in the hotel.'

'You're doing well lad, don't stop now, what about Mrs Celia Bellamy?'

'My word sir, you don't look at ladies legs do you? I've

never seen her wear any. She's quite dark and her legs are tanned. Mind you, she'll probably have to start wearing support tights now that she's expecting. My wife had to, to help her varicose veins.'

'Roper, you certainly know a lot about women.' the sergeant smiled proudly.

'But it's just occurred to me, could it have been a man wearing tights or a stocking over his face and Mr Cranmore tried to remove it.'

'I never thought of that' said Roper 'I was thinking he had a woman in car, made advances to her, she pulled away and he caught his hand on her tights . . . . only there wasn't any evidence of a woman being in the car was there?'

* * *

The doorbell of Janet Morgan's house rang as Pc Lewis stood on the doorstep.

'Come in, I've been expecting you.'

After the usual introductions the young Pc said 'I've just come to get a statement from you to confirm that Mrs Richards was with you last Sunday evening.'

'Yes, that's right. I haven't seen her for a while, it was nice for us to have one of our little get togethers.'

'Can you remember what time she arrived?'

'Yes, she was a little early, it was eight fifteen pm.'

'Are you sure of that time?'

'I'm certain. I'd put a bottle of white wine in the

fridge, as us girls must have our tipple you know? She smiled. 'Anyway, I was watching the television and in the adverts I went to get the wine out and the doorbell rang, it was eight fifteen pm, she said she's be with me at about eight thirty pm.'

'And she left at?' the Pc was busy writing.

'Oh about eleven o'clock I think.'

'Well thank you very much Mrs Morgan, you've been very helpful.'

'Oh good. Rosemary's been through such a lot lately with all the problems of the hotel, it did her good to get away for a few hours . . . don't hesitate to call me if you need any help.

Now can I get you a drink, cup of tea . . . . or something stronger.

'Not on duty . . . but a cup of tea would be appreciated. Thank you.'

✳ ✳ ✳

George was red in the face. He slammed the building Society book down on the table.

'What are these withdrawals Rosemary?'

'Oh George, you're so melodramatic.'

'Look, same amount every month. You're being blackmailed aren't you?'

Rosemary laughed 'and you say I read too many detective novels.'

'You've been really anxious lately, worried about

business in the hotel and all of a sudden you're not bothered. You let me do the accounts that night you went to Janet's, why? You never let me near them normally, you always insist on doing them yourself and you never even checked them. What's going on?'

'Alright George, calm down and I'll tell you . . . '

'Well it had better be good that's all I can say.'

※ ※ ※

Inspector Trafford was going through Janet Morgan's statement with Pc Lewis.

'And you're sure she was certain of the times?'

'Yes sir, apparently Mrs Richards was a little early, she told Mrs Morgan she wouldn't be there till 8.30pm.'

'Right thanks a lot, that will be all for now. The Pc left.

※ ※ ※

Inspector Trafford plugged his kettle in and looked out of the window deep in thought.

Mrs Richards had left the house at six thirty pm according to her husband, it would have only of taken fifteen to twenty minutes to get from Babbacombe to this side of the river Dart where Mrs Morgan lived. She wouldn't have to get the ferry over so it was possible that Mrs Richards could have been with Dave Cranmore that evening, even killed him but surely she knew her alibi would be checked. She wouldn't be able to bluff her way out of losing two hours. He'd have to speak to her about it.

Just then Roper entered the office.

'Kettle's boiling!'

'What?'

'Kettle's boiling sir.'

'Oh yes, okay'

He started to make the tea.

'Any luck with questioning the locals and guest houses in Babbacombe yet?'

'Well it's all in hand but nothings come to light.'

'I could have organised that anyway' said Roper 'Instead of you putting the station lads on it.'

'You're more valuable to me here. Besides, i've got to give some of these young Pc's a bit of responsibility; far too many leaving the force nowadays.'

'Mmm I suppose you're right' Roper shrugged his shoulders. 'Mind you, it's normally dark at that time I don't know if anyone would have noticed anything.'

'I disagree' said Inspector Trafford 'Lots of people go for a walk in the early evening especially the hotel and guest house proprietors. They are quiet at this time of the year and there's a lot of retired people in Babbacombe. It's a quiet place compared to Torquay. Still, I'm sure somebody would have noticed something.'

❊ ❊ ❊

The Inspector's car drove up the to the Sherwell Hotel and it's tyres crunched to a halt on the gravel.

'Steady there Roper. You'll rip the tyres to ribbons, besides I wanted to surprise them. I think the whole neighbourhood have heard us arrive.'

Mary showed them into the lounge and went to get Mrs Richards.

'Hello Inspector, Sergeant. I didn't expect you today, I don't think anyone's here.'

'It's you want I want to speak to actually Mrs Richards.'

'Oh okay, have a seat.' She straightened her skirt and sat down.'

'We went to see your friend Janet Morgan to confirm the time that you arrived and she says you didn't get there until eight fifteen pm. I believe you left the house at six thirty pm. Can you account for those two hours Mrs Richards?'

'Well I went for a walk along the beach. I must have lost track of the time I suppose' she nervously fiddled with her hair.

'Come come now Mrs Richards, you're an intelligent woman. Surely you can't expect us to believe that two hours are unaccounted for. You have no alibi.'

'Sometimes I need to get away by myself, I've had a lot on my mind lately.'

'I can appreciate that' said the Inspector 'But you told your friend you wouldn't be there until 8.30pm so you must have known in advance that you wouldn't be going straight there, it wasn't a spur of the moment decision. Mr Cranmore was killed that evening. You would have had ample time to get from Babbacombe to your friends house.'

'So you think I murdered Dave . . . I loved him like a brother . . . How could you think such a thing?'

'Well can you account for those two hours?'

'Well, yes . . . I mean no, I went for a walk.'

'You'll have to do better than that Mrs Richards. It's either here or at the station.'

'Well I suppose it's got to come out sometime . . . I'll just get Mary to make us some tea.'

She came back after a few minutes.

'Well Inspector, this is how it all began . . .'

✳ ✳ ✳

The following day Roper was in the office sifting through reports from Mr Hounslow's accountant that the Inspector had sent for.

'Anything there Roper?'

'Well apparently he had bought into this Owners Abroad, Home Ownership and they had gone into liquidation, he had lost quite a lot of capital. It wasn't surplus. He'd taken it out of a firm in Germany that he was doing business with and they were putting pressure on him, so it's always possible he could have murdered his mother to get him out of a fix.'

'I think if he'd have approached her and told her the

truth about the position he was in she would have bailed him out, but probably have taken over that side of business and taken money out of one of his other assets to teach him a lesson. She wouldn't let him get away with anything but it was as much in her interest as his to keep things running smoothly.'

'So nothing there then you think?'

'No but we'll ask him about it. It might put the wind up him, perhaps he'll let something slip. But I really believe he was genuinely fond of his mother. Do you think I'm becoming a softie Roper, seeing too much good in people?'

'No way, you don't let me get away with anything!'

Inspector Trafford laughed.

'You know what they say sir, charity begins at work!'

＊ ＊ ＊

Peter was in the garden at the Sherwell Hotel doing a bit of pruning for Tom.

Sylvia came out and sat on a nearby bench.

'Oh Peter, I thought only pensioners and old spinsters liked gardening?'

'I feel I'm getting closer to nature when I'm in the garden. You ought to try it sometime Sylvia, it's quite theraputic.'

'It would play havoc with my nails.'

She held a perfectly manicured hand up to examine her nails and her rings glistened in the sun. 'Anyway if you want to get closer to nature, you could always lay your green fingers on me!'

She walked up to him as he was kneeling down. He glanced up at perfectly formed limbs in black stockings and caught sight of the fleshy bit of leg at the top of her suspenders. He suddenly put his hand up her skirt and grabbed the top of her leg.

'You should keep away from me Sylvia, you're too much of a temptation.'

He put pressure on her leg.

'Peter, you're hurting me' a look of pain passed over her face.

'You know I like a bit of sadism' he pushed her against the tree and kissed her face and neck passionately as his fingers went inside her blouse and grabbed her breast. As he looked up, her face went from one of pleasure to horror as she looked over his shoulder. Celia stood behind them.

'Martha was right! She was right all along, but I would not believe her and to think what I've done.'

'Darling it's not what you think.' He suddenly pushed Sylvia away. She lost her balance and fell straight into the mud as Peter ran after Celia.

She locked herself in their bedroom and refused to let him in.

Peter went to George and Simon and quickly told them what had happened making sure he left out certain details.

'I must have that skeleton key to get in the room

George.' He sounded very anxious.

'I wouldn't bother' said Simon 'Let her stew, it will do her good.'

'I don't know whether I ought to give it to you.'

'Look George, Rosemary won't let me have the keys, Celia's in a terrible state, she may do herself some harm and what with the baby and everything.'

George gave in and handed him the keys. Peter raced upstairs and let himself in the room.

Celia was packing her case.

'I was warned about you and I didn't believe it, but now?'

'Who by?'

'Martha.'

'Oh she'd condemn anybody.'

'Would she? There's no smoke without fire!'

'But I love you' Peter said 'And what about the baby?'

'You should have thought of that when you decided to mess around with that woman!'

'That's all she is, that woman, she threw herself at me, I'm only human. It was pure lust, I grabbed her to play her up, there was no real feeling in it. You are the only woman I love.'

'Sure, I've heard it all before. I'm off.'

Peter fell to his knees. 'You can't go, I need you, Celia please . . .'

* * *

Inspector Trafford was working out how much he had got to pick up from the local bookmakers. He wasn't what you'd call a gambling man but he did like a little flutter now and again if it was a special horse race, or he'd been given a tip and he would always take his wife with him to his annual visit to Cheltenham every March and they would stay overnight and make a short break of it. He was totting up the last amount when Roper came in.

'I checked with the mobile unit on the cars you asked for.'

'Hang on a minute nearly finished . . . thirty five pounds, not bad, but it would have been more if I'd have paid tax.'

'Does that mean you are going to treat me to a drink after work?'

'I'll consider it, it all depends if you've got anything for me.' he grinned. 'Now we discussed the other night about trying to find how the murderer got to Babbacombe. Keeping to our main suspects at the hotel there's Mr Hounslow's red Jaguar I should imagine that would be easy to spot. Mrs Richards drives a cream 'C' reg Rover. Mr and Mrs Turley don't have a car and Peter and Celia Bellamy have a blue Sierra

'Well none have those have been sighted. I've given the registrations and descriptions of the cars to the lads at the mobile unit and they have interviewed the local people but nobody has noticed anything.'

Inspector Trafford scratched his head. 'I didn't think

we would have any joy there Roper. There's so many cars about nowadays. I mean unless it's a very unusual or a classy car, people don't really notice them. What about the taxi firms?'

'I've interviewed all the local firms and the taxis at the harbour to see if any fares were booked to Babbacombe on that night, there were people being dropped to the theatre, but nothing's come to light I'm afraid.'

'I don't think you will be getting that drink then Roper. What about the buses?'

'Well there is that little open top bus that goes to Babbacombe. I've checked with them but they can't recall anything unusual.'

'So did the murderer come in Dave Cranmore's car and yet forensic say not, or did they walk there? Let's check for taxis and buses leaving Babbacombe to see if anyone was spotted.'

'Okay sir, I'll get onto it now.'

'Oh by the way. We've got a statement from the man whose boat Simon Turley fell off and he confirmed he'd seen the entire incident and he wasn't pushed over. He seems to be quite a genuine sort of a bloke. He's lived here for years I think he's reliable.'

'Oh well . . . that's at least one more thing out of the way.' The Inspector sounded slightly pleased.

He left the office and Inspector Trafford got out the statement made by Mrs Richards. Apparently she had borrowed money off the late Mrs Hounslow for the hotel.

That's probably why, according to Mr Richards, Mrs Hounslow was interfering in the running of it. It wasn't an official contract. Mrs Richards was just paying her back in monthly instalments, that had accounted for the withdrawals in her building society book. So according to Mrs Richards, she wasn't being blackmailed by Dave, the idea of which she found ludicrous. She had hated the arrangement and felt that Martha had control over her, and was meddling in the affairs of the hotel. She had found it hard to restrain herself from a full scale confrontation with her, and yet she couldn't go to the banks because the interest rates were so high. She had felt trapped, until a solicitor friend, a Mr Jaffrey, had offered to lend her the money to clear the debt which was about four thousand pounds, and Rosemary would pay him back when she could.

'Sounds like a good friend, sure nothing's going on there' Roper had suggested.

According to Mrs Richards, she and George had helped him when his wife had been very ill and had since passed away, and it was his way of returning the favour.

Mrs Richards was released from her debt due to Martha's death. There had been no legal contract so she no longer needed to borrow money from him and she had been to tell him on the way to Janet Morgan's house, that's why she was late arriving.

Mr Jaffray had confirmed her story. His late wife and himself had known George and Rosemary before they'd moved to Torquay and he had dealt with the conveyancing of the hotel for them but Inspector Trafford was still a little doubtful in case there had been something going on between them and he was lying for her.

He had thought that perhaps four thousand pounds was not a lot of money not by todays standards, but if it was a threat to Mrs Richards hotel or livelihood in some way perhaps she could kill for it.

She loved Torquay and she loved the Sherwell Hotel. Did Martha stand in the way of her losing everything? Surely not. As a last resort she could have gone to any bank or had Martha Hounslow got some other hold on her that had not come to light?

Inspector Trafford was finding this case difficult. They always say find the personality of the victim and you have found the killer, but nobody except for her son like Mrs Hounslow.

Was George Richards involved? He seemed a boring sort of husband but those are sometimes the most genuine. Would he have killed for his wife's sake?

Sylvia hated Martha and vice-versa. William loved his mother, yes he believed that, but the money he would inherit . . .

He was a reasonably rich man before his mother's death, but now he might never need to work again.

Dave Cranmore – surely he had not killed her – the fact that he had been murdered excluded him. A wheeler-dealer, yes, but a murderer?

Then Peter Bellamy, she knew a lot about him. So what if his wife had found out about his philandering from Martha Hounslow. Surely he would have been able to sweet talk his way out of it. He had had plenty of practice with his lady friends.

His wife . . . possible. Seems a charming woman, but how knows?

Simon Turley. Well possibly the only thing he would kill for would be a fishing rod, or did he know the real Simon or was this obsession with fishing an exaggeration.

Mavis Turley, the timid mouse. Surely she couldn't hurt a fly, but neither could some hardened criminals.

Inspector Trafford was perplexed and in a quandry.

When Roper came in he said 'Put your coat on, I have decided to splash out with my winnings after all.'

※ ※ ※

A pair of red lips pursed in front of the dressing table mirror.

'Mmm I rather like this shade' she said as she carefully blotted them on a tissue.

'Never mind the bloody lipstick what do you say?'

'Oh the divorce. Yes, I don't mind William, as long as I get a good settlement. We will have to have a legal separation, the only thing that is worrying me is that we have got a good social life. I wonder whether we will get invited out to so many meals and functions if they know we're no longer together. Do you think it will be bad for business?'

'Uh, that's rich. Whenever have you worried about what's bad for business?'

'Well I wouldn't want it going down the drain, I mean I'm entitled to half when we divorce.'

'I might have guessed. anyway I might let Jeffries handle things at work for a while.'

Sylvia looked amazed.

'You normally like to have your finger on the button. You have never trusted anyone else to run things.'

'Well Jeffries is quite capable and trustworthy, he's got a good business head on his shoulders.'

'I know that' said Sylvia. 'But apparently you didn't think he could cope a few months back when you had a bad bout of flu and dragged yourself in with a temperature.'

'I know that was stupid of me, but he's going to have to cope because I'm going on a holiday when all this is finished.'

'Holiday, you've had a holiday here, if you can call it that.' What's wrong with you William?'

'Oh do what you like . . . .' He stormed out slamming the bedroom door behind him.

✳ ✳ ✳

Roper was just tucking into his third bag of cheese and onion crisps.

'I can't understand why you don't put any weight on
. . . and I dread to think what you're breath will smell
like after those.' said Inspector Trafford.

'I'll tell you one thing, these crisps give you a thirst.'

'You'd better get another one in then hadn't you?' the
Inspector pushed his empty glass towards him.

Just then the phone rang on the bar. The landlord
stretched his neck to look over the heads of the people
queueing at the bar and he caught sight of Inspector
Trafford sitting in the corner.

'John' he shouted. 'Call for you.'

Inspector Trafford made his way to the bar, with all
the row and chatter around him could barely hear the
speaker on the other end but eventually he fathomed
out, despite the din that the team searching the top of
Babbacombe had found a small leather bobble that's
normally on the ends of lace up shoes. It might be
important but they'd put in a sealed container and were
bringing it over to him.

He was just about to call Roper but decided to leave
him to it. He was sure he would have managed two pints
as he wasn't driving so he left the pub alone.

* * *

He examined it closely. It was a small leather navy
blue bobble that's put on the ends of laces on the more
expensive ladies shoes.

'I suppose it could just have been a passerby. It might

not be linked to the murderer at all.'

Still he thought he would have to check the shoes of the ladies at the hotel.

The following day, Roper asked him why he had left the pub without telling him. Inspector Trafford explained about the shoe lace.

'Well you could have finished your pint sir . . . by the way didn't Mr Hounslow say that Mavis was wearing some old lace up shoes the night he met her?'

'Yes, we'll go to the Sherwell later and check, although these leather bobbles are normally found on expensive shoes, doesn't seem like the type she would wear. And we didn't find any shoes like that when we searched all the bedrooms, did we Roper?'

'No. Sylvia Hounslow has got all high heeled shoes. Mrs Richards hadn't any blue lace-ups, neither had Celia Bellamy or Mavis Turley, unless they had hid them.'

'But why should they hide them Roper? When we searched all the rooms, were were investigating Martha Hounslows death not Dave Cranmore's. The shoes would have been unimportant then. Now if we searched them now and they have been hidden that would be understandable if they had been worn at his murder.'

'So why didn't we find Mrs Turley's lace-up shoes when we searched her room?'

'Well we were not looking for shoes then, they may have been there and we didn't notice them or she could have been wearing them at the time.'

They returned to the hotel and were taken into the individual bedrooms of Sylvia Hounslow, Celia and Mrs Richards room.

Just as they had expected Sylvia had no 'sensible shoes' at all in her vast collection.

Mrs Richards had two pairs of walking shoes, neither of which matched up to the navy lace bobble. Celia had a pair of lace-up shoes that were rather new as she had only purchased them that week from a shop in Torquay. She said because they were comfortable and would see her through the pregnancy.

Mavis Turley produced the shoes she had worn on the night she had met William, a black suede pair. She looked rather embarrassed as they were worn and down at heel.

'I have got better shoes you know Inspector. I mean nothing compared to the ones Sylvia wears,but better than these.It's just that as I was meeting William on Meadfoot beach, I thought we would be walking and there was no point in putting on a good pair, although I was rather embarrassed when he took me to that nice restaurant.'

'I'm sure you looked as nice as anyone in there.' Inspector Trafford lied. 'Tell me Mrs Turley, do you recognise this?'

He placed the navy bobble in front of her.

'No . . . I've never seen any shoes with a bobble like that on the lace. Sorry I can't be of more help.'

Inspector Trafford asked the same questions of the

other three ladies, but none of them recalled seeing any navy shoes with bobbled lace-ups.

They interviewed Mary and Lil before they left and they both said the same.

'Of course we haven't searched their homes.' said Roper. 'Do you think there's any need?'

'We can't leave any stone unturned.' Inspector Trafford replied. 'I'll send PC Lewis round.'

* * *

Inspector Trafford and Roper were back at the office.

'So no-one in the hotel owns a pair of shoes of that description unless it's a man with a very small foot'. he laughed.

'Well let's just say Roper we couldn't find them. Anyone of the ladies could be the owner of the shoes and if they were the murderer they might get rid of them.'

'But they'd have to realise that a bobble was missing and think they may have left it at the scene of the crime, because if they had not noticed they wouldn't think it necessary to dispose of the shoes.'

'I think it's a long shot Roper but get the dustbins checked, though I'm sure they wouldn't dispose of them locally. I think we will check with the men to see if they remember any of the ladies owning shoes of that description.'

'If they could, would they mention it. If it was their own wife she might have warned them not to say anything, but she had have to tell them why.' suggested Roper.

Inspector Trafford sat in a pensive mood for a few minutes.

'Well you know Roper, you could have hit on something there. We keep saying we're looking for a murderer but how about if the murderer had an accomplice and they are working as a couple?'

'Well if that's the case we can't bank on the reliability of the interviews if they were lying to protect each other.'

'Yes, I mean we have been given information, some we can check out, the rest could be a load of lies. The only thing people can't really hide unless they are very clever is their true personality. Maybe we have got to look at that.'

CHAPTER SEVENTEEN

A fortunate fare

The following day they finally had a break through. a taxi driver, Joe Dowding from the 'Harbour Taxis' had said he'd picked up a fare from Babbacombe at approximately eight pm on the night of the murder.

So Inspector Trafford had him brought into the station to make a statement.

'Now Mr. Dowding, thank you for coming. Please take a seat.' He switched on the tape recorder. 'and gave details of the time and date.'

'I hope this won't take long. I mean business is bad at the moment. We work on a rota system down at the harbour. I could be missing some good fares.'

'It shouldn't take too long, but this is a murder investigation. Now you say you picked up a fare from Babbacombe. Was it booked?'

'No, what happened was I had collected a retired couple from the Princess theatre at about seven fifteen pm and had driven them to the Hotel Regent on the front at Babbacombe at approximately seven thirty-five pm.'

'Does it normally take twenty minutes?'

'No only the man was a bit frail and it took me a while getting him in and out of the car. They gave me a tip though, so I didn't mind. You don't get much tipping nowadays. Don't get many fares come to that.'

'Anyway, carry on.'

'Well there was a tea stand up by the cable lift.'

'Yes, I recall the lads at the unit checking with the man who runs it to see if he'd seen anything unusual' Roper said to Inspector Trafford.

'Anyway, this woman comes up to me, looks a little flushed and asks me if I'm booked. I said No and asked her where she would liked to go and she thought for a minute and said the harbour.'

'Can you describe her to me?'

'Well I have loads of passengers and I would normally have found that difficult, but I noticed that she had lovely red hair. Of course my wife used to be red in her younger days and I've always had a soft spot for redheads. You can keep your bottled blondes.'

'Er yes precisely . . . Now can you tell us anything else about her?' Inspector Trafford didn't want to rush him, he seemed the type to like to go at his own pace and he didn't want him to clam up, but at the same time he was getting rather anxious and excited.

'Well she had a mac on and that's about it, I think.'

'Well how old was she . . . thirties, forties, fifties?'

'It's difficult to say with women. Possibly late thirties. Oh and she wore sort of tinted glasses.'

'Sunglasses?'

'No. You know the ones with tinted lenses.'

'Yes I know the type. They are quite fashionable.' Roper informed the Inspector.

'So you didn't see the colour of her eyes?'

'Well no, not with the glasses on.'

'And did you happen to notice what shoes she was wearing?'

'Shoes . . . No, it's something I wouldn't have looked at.'

'Did you have your back to her when she came up?' asked Inspector Trafford.

'Let me think . . . Yes I did, I was talking to the Cafe owner.'

'So you wasn't aware she was approaching you?'

'No I don't suppose I was' he looked confused.

'Was the tea van parked on the grass?'

'No on the road.'

'So would she have to walk over the grass to get to you?'

'I think she came along the pavement, but I can't see what you are getting at.'

'Not to worry' said Inspector Trafford 'Would you like a cup of tea?'

'Yes I'd love one, thanks. Will it take much longer?'

'No, have your tea and we'll finished taking your

statement afterwards.' He switched off the tape recorder after a short message and sent a Pc into the room. He and Roper left to get themselves and Joe Dowding some tea.

'What was all that about?' inquired Roper.

Inspector Trafford sounded jubilant. 'Well if she was wearing high heels, he would have heard her coming along the pavement wouldn't he?'

'Of course, I can hear my wife coming a mile off, clip clopping when she's wearing her high heels. Well done Sir.'

'Well it maybe a long shot Roper, but there's a chance she was wearing flat shoes because he didn't hear her.'

'And what about the red hair. I mean Mrs Richards had got red hair although she's got flecks of grey in hers. He didn't mention the grey.'

'Come on, we'll get the tea.'

'You mean your having the canteen rubbish?' said Roper.

I'll have to put with it this time.'

They took Joe Dowding his tea and he asked if he could smoke.

He lit a cigarette. They switched on the tape recorder and the interview continued.

'Now you say red hair. Was it bright red hair?'

'Well . . . yes . . . no it was a lovely titian colour.'

'And was there any grey?'

'Well I didn't notice.'

'And the style, what was the style like?' Inspector

Trafford began to get excited.

'It was long. Lovely long locks flowing down her back.'

His face dropped. Mrs Richards hair was just passed her chin.

'Think carefully, is there anything else you can remember? What clothes was she wearing?' Roper asked.

'As far as I can remember, just a long coat . . . a raincoat I think . . . Yes sort of beigy . . . .cream . . . that's about it. Oh yes and she was carrying a shopping bag.'

'Have you cleaned the car since that day?'

'No I haven't. It doesn't get that dirty at this time of the year. In the summer when I take family fares, they've always got sand over their feet and then I have to clean it every couple of days. I think I just brushed the seats and sprayed it with air freshener.'

'Well we will have to take your car down to forensic and have it examined.'

'Now wait a minute, I haven't done anything wrong, and need that car for work. I can't afford to be without it. I've got two teenage kids in college . . . If you knew how much they cost to keep,'

'We're not saying you've done anything wrong, we just think there's a possibility that a murder suspect may have used your car. We should only need it for about twenty four hours. we'll get it back to you as soon as possible and you wouldn't want to hinder us in our investigations. We are talking about a brutal murder. You do want to help your local police don't you?' asked Inspector Trafford.

'Oh well, yes of course' the taxi driver looked unsure.

'I can assure you that we'll try not to disrupt your routine or work anymore than is necessary. I've got a family myself and I know what an expense they can be. Of course mine are only small yet.' Roper added.

'Well it get worse believe me . . . there's college books, bus passes . . . .'

'Well yes we won't keep you any longer.' Inspector Trafford wanted to wind up the interview.

'Roper, can you arrange a lift home for Mr. Dowding. We'll contact you the moment your car has been released from forensic and please don't hesitate to let us know if you remember anything else no matter how minor.'

Sergeant Roper got things moving and arranged for the car to be collected that day and sent straight to forensic.

Inspector Trafford was hoping for some sort of a lead from this although he was doubtful but it seemed the only thing he had to go on. And yet the description didn't fit anyone in the hotel, unless there was an outsider involved in the murder that they knew nothing about.

There was no joy when the forensic had search Martha Hounslow's room. No red hairs found then, in fact nothing was discovered that could shed any light on who had put the Digoxin in the bottle of Magnesia.

Anyone could have gone into the room although it was sometimes locked. Mary had a skeleton key when she cleaned the rooms, and so did Mr and Mrs Richards. Anyone could have got hold of it or Mrs Hounslow could have left her room open. No, there was no joy there at all. They had to keep looking for clues in the second murder and there was no doubt that the two were connected.

CHAPTER EIGHTEEN

Charity begins at home

Inspector Trafford looked over at his wife as he laid down his knife and fork.

'That was lovely Betty' he finished the last of his red wine.

'Any cheese and biscuits?' he grinned.

'There's a bit of Stilton left.'

'Good. I'll get that last drop of Port out.' he got up and walked to the cabinet.

'All this drink will dull your brain, you'll have a hangover tomorrow' his wife said as she place the cheese board on the table.

'I don't think it can get any duller, dear.'

'Things not looking too good then?'

'Well we may have a lead with this taxi driver. We're checking his car out. There may be a connection on a fare he picked up.'

'What sort of person is responsible for the murders John?'

'Well they are either very clever and one step ahead of us all the time, or they are not smart at all. No actually, I don't mean that they are dumb, just an ordinary person and maybe they have not worked every detail out but they have just got luck on their side, and they have done it so simple, there's nothing intricate for us to solve. Anyway, enough about me, how was you day?'

'Well I had a few games of bowls with Audrey this morning and I did a couple of hours in the Charity shop this afternoon as Mrs Biddle wasn't well. You would be amazed at the things that people bring in. We had a sailor's uniform, a checked table cloth and a pair of china dogs brought in today. I quite liked the dogs, but I knew you would go mad.'

'Well we have got enough ornaments don't you think?'

'Mind you, you'd be surprised at the rubbish some people bring in. I suppose they just can't bear to throw anything away.'

'Waste not want not' the Inspector said as he polished off the last piece of cheese.

'Mind you, we have got more staff than customers at the moment.'

'Well they all work for nothing don't they?' the Inspector said as he filled his glass with port.

'Well they do have the first choice of the things that come in, but they do it because they are lonely. some of them are widows, or they are married and their children have moved away. They have just got too much time on their hands.'

'Ugh, I wish I could say the same. Never enough hours in the day. Do you need a hand with the washing up?'

'No you're alright, I mean after all, now our children have left, I have got all the time in the world. The washing up will give me something to do!' She playfully threw a tea towel at him as he retreated to the garden.

'I think I will trim that conifer down a bit' he thought and went to get his shears out of the shed. He saw a butterfly flit past. 'Escape, escape' why did those words suddenly come to him. A small glass phial. He had seen it somewhere but where? He just couldn't think and yet he felt it had some sort of connection to the case. A small phial with a rubber top, and the shoes, his mind kept going back to the shoes. Hadn't someone somewhere mentioned shoes.

✳ ✳ ✳

The information came in from forensic the next day. they had gone over the car with a fine tooth comb. No sign of any leather bobbles which they were hoping for, but the red hairs found on the back seat were synthetic not human hair.

'So the passenger wore a wig, obviously to hide their identity' Roper said thoughtfully.

'I would think so, I mean I know women wear them

for appearance sake if their own hair is thinning or a mess, but in this case with the tinted glasses as well, I think we can safely assume it was a disguise.'

'Do you think we ought to get Mr Dowding to look at the women at the Sherwell sir, to see if he can identify any of them?'

'Yes we will have to arrange it, although if the person was heavily disguised, it might not be very successful.'

'Well what about the voice. Could he perhaps spot that? A Midland accent for instance, although he must speak to locals or passengers throughout the day, maybe he doesn't take much notice of their voices.'

'But he may spot a Midland accent against a Devon one.'

'Of course there is one thing we are forgetting aren't we? It could have been a man!'

'Quite possible Roper, we will speak to Mr Dowding again.'

'Shall I arrange another search of the hotel for the wig and the tinted glasses?'

'We'll have to. Although I can't see that we will have any success there. They would have got rid of them by now. Still' we'll get all the litter bins and skips searched around the harbour where he or she left the taxi just in case they were dumped there. Also, we'll get all the wig shops and hairdressers checked locally to see if anyone has purchased a wig of that description lately. Oh and the costume hire shop.

'The trouble with those is that you normally hire the

wig or costume for twenty four hours and then they have to be returned or you don't get your deposit back and you have to leave your name and address, so it doesn't seem likely that they'd have got it from there.'

'No that's a good point Roper. Still check it all the same and I'll tell you what, check out all the charity shops.'

'Oxfam Sue Ryder all those you mean?' Roper looked confused.

'Yes my wife says they sell the most unusual things. Someone could have bought it from there.'

'Okay sir, I'll get on to it straight away.'

In the meantime, Inspector Trafford arranged to have another word with Mr Dowding. He said he hadn't detected any sort of accent, although the person hardly spoke and he was quite annoyed when the Inspector suggested, that it could possibly have been a man.

'I've been married years Inspector. I have also been to drag shows with my mates. No man could fool me. It was definitely a woman.'

When the Inspector informed him that the hairs found in the car were synthetic, Mr Dowding didn't seem shocked.

'Actually Inspector, although I have got a thing about red hair, as I told you, I must admit it did seem rather thick and immaculate for human hair.'

Later that day, Inspector Trafford arranged for Mr Dowding to go with him to the hotel.

Rosemary answered the door. They met Lil and Mary

and later he met Celia, Mavis and Sylvia. He said it was difficult due to the wig and glasses, but as far as he could tell nobody there was the person that he had picked up in the taxi.

As they were driving back, the Inspector turned to him. 'Are you sure now Mr Dowding?' the Inspector sounded rather earnest. 'What about the voices?'

'I'm sure the cook was far too big. That little kitchen girl was too short. I wouldn't have forgotten the blonde, nice bit of stuff eh? She would never have disguised a figure like that, wig or no wig. The dark lady, no, the skin colouring was wrong and the little sweet lady, Mavis Turley you said. No her voice was soft and timid.'

'And what about the owner Mrs Richards?

'Ah the red head. Pleasant enough she was, but no it wasn't her I'm sure.

They dropped him off.

'Well thanks Mr Dowding, you can have your car back tomorrow' Roper said.

'Oh good, and I'm sorry I couldn't have been more help.'

'We will be in touch if we need you again.'

'Any luck at the hairdressers or wig shops?' The inspector asked solemnly as they drove off.

'Need you ask?' said Roper.

'We'll just pop back to the station for an hour and then you can get off home.'

They passed the front desk. Sergeant Blundon called them.

'Oh Inspector, there is a note on your desk from Pc Lewis, something about the local Oxfam shop.'

'Oh really, another red herring I suppose.' The Inspector grunted as he went to his office.

'That's not like John' the sergeant said to Roper.

'It's this case, it's getting him down.'

Roper walked into the office and Inspector Trafford was beaming. He was holding a piece of paper in his hand.

'Don't tell me' said Roper 'The local Oxfam shop has sold a red wig to someone.'

'Well that would have been a bit of good information, but this is great.'

'Well don't keep me in suspense, what is it?'

'Well Pc Lewis went into the local Oxfam shop to see if they had sold a red wig, they hadn't but they were sorting through the stuff that had come in, and a red wig had been brought in.'

'Where is it now?' asked Roper.

'Forensic have got it. Let's go and see them.'

Forensic confirmed the hairs found in the taxi matched exactly to the wig, even though they were synthetic, the length and colour matched perfectly.

'So you don't think it could be a coincidence?' said Roper.'Well how many wigs like this are going around Torquay?' the Inspector replied.

When they got back to the office, Pc Lewis gave the Inspector the details of the shop in Union Road. They left immediately.

The manageress, a Mrs Cummings, took the Inspector to a small elderly lady called Miss Twigg.

Apparently Miss Twig was responsible for all the goods that came into the shop. If they were in a bad state and they couldn't be sold, they were thrown out. Clothes were pressed and put on hangers and when they was ready Mrs Cummings would price them.

'So you do see the people that bring the things into the shop?'

'Well most times I do. Sometimes they just leave the bag on the counter and go.'

'Can you remember who brought the wig in?'

'Oh yes, a pleasant young lady. She gave me a carrier bag. It had a wig and a pair of shoes it, and a small bottle.'

Inspector Trafford became anxious.

'Have you still got the shoes?'

'Well I think they are on display if we haven't already sold them.'

They went to a rack of shoes neatly stacked with white stickers on them – one pound, one pound fifty, two pounds. Miss Twigg went over and pointed to a pair of navy shoes with laces on. There were two bobbles on the one shoe and none on the other.

Inspector Trafford hugged the little old lady and kissed her on the forehead.

'Oh really, I mean . . . ' she looked pleased, and embarrassed.

'Do forgive me dear Lady, not a very responsible

thing for an Inspector to do.' He took her hand apologetically.

That's alright Inspector, at my age one doesn't get kissed by many young men.'

Mrs Twigg was late seventies she could easily have been his mother.

'When you say the lady that brought them in was young, how old do you mean?'

'Oh forties or younger, I'm not quite sure.'

'I can't tell you what a tremendous help you've been Miss Twigg. This could help us in a murder enquiry.'

She looked very pleased.

'I bet it's the highlight of her day coming in here sorting out other people's cast offs' thought Roper.

She looked a little pale and began to sway. Roper quickly got her a chair.

'Are you alright?' Mrs Cummings came over 'Miss Twigg isn't used to this sort of excitement Inspector' she said sharply.

'I'm alright really, nothing exciting has ever happened to me, except when the war was on. Please, I'm fine, perhaps a cup of tea?'

'I'll go and make us some' said Mrs Cummings.

'That would be lovely' said Inspector Trafford. 'Now are you sure that you are Okay?'

'Yes fine. I may be small but I'm tough'.

'Now did you say there was a bottle?'

'Oh yes, a small glass dropper with a rubber top, you know the sort people use for eye drops or ear drops, but

I have thrown it out. Mind you, the dustbins are only outside.'

'Roper go out and have a look.'

Roper came in after a few minutes with the bottle and he carefully placed it in a polythene bag.

'Oh I'm sorry, I shouldn't have thrown it out. Is it important? Only we couldn't have sold it?'

'I should say it was vital' said Inspector Trafford. It was the bottle that he'd had on his mind on for a week.

Mrs Cummings brought the tea in on a tray.

'Now you've been a tremendous help Miss Twigg but we may need you to identify the lady that brought these things in.'

'Of course I will' said Miss Twigg sipping her tea.

The Inspector told Roper to take a statement and a full description of the woman.

'Although I don't need it!'

Roper looked shocked.

'I know who it is Roper, it's been staring me in the face.'

Later that day after Roper had got a description and statement from Miss Twigg he went to Inspector Trafford's office. He looked bemused.

'This bottle, I can't see the significance of it!'

'Can't you Roper, I believe that it was used to put the weed killer in Martha Hounslow's mussel sauce. You imagine how easy it would be to walk past and just squeeze the rubber top and two or three drops quickly go into the starter. It could easily have been hidden up the sleeve. It's only small and it would only take seconds. Even if it had been swilled out there would still be traces of the weed killer or a similar substance. I've no doubt that forensic will confirm this.'

'But, I still don't know who the murderer is.'

'Well it will have to be proven, unless of course they break down and confess. But all the facts fit.'

'Yes, but is there a motive?'

'Well there is Roper, but not one that you might understand, but me being a middle aged man, I can appreciate how someone could be driven to it.'

'But what can we do without definite proof?'

'We will have a few statements to go on and Miss Twigg will hopefully be able to identify who came in to the shop.'

'God, I wish I knew who you were talking about!'

'You'll find out tonight. I'm arranging for a meeting at the house.'

'Do you think we will need any back up Sir?'

'I wouldn't think so Roper, still maybe we'll take some just in case.'

※ ※ ※

'Well I have enjoyed myself, I don't know about anyone else?' Simon sat back in the deckchair and lit a cigarette.

Rosemary turned round towards him with a trowel in her hand she was weeding the flower bed, she looked a little disgusted.

'How can you say that Simon, we have had two deaths since you have been down here. Honestly, you men, you're so insensitive!'

'Insensitive eh! Well tell me this, why did you move down here?'

'I'd had enough of the city, I've always wanted to live by the sea.'

'Precisely! Well I'm stuck in factory all year round, I hardly ever see the sun or get any fresh air except when I go fishing. This has been a real break for me despite what's happened. It beats an eight still six shift on a machine anyday. I mean, Mavis only does a few hours a day at the Home for the elderly and the rest of the time is her own.'

'Well for once I think you are right Simon, I couldn't go back to the Midlands to live. I suppose sometimes you take it for granted living by the sea, it's only when you think you might lose it all and have to move that you realise just how much it means to you. Of course it's been a change for you despite what has happened, I shouldn't have said that.'

'Well I will forgive you if you go and get me a drink' he smiled.

She got up and brushed the hair from her face.

'Okay, you can finish the weeding while I fetch it.' She shoved the trowel in his hand. 'If you want a drink you'll have to earn it!'

'And you say that men are insensitive' he got up from

his deckchair 'I thought this was Tom's job' he shouted after her as she disappeared into the hotel.

She bumped into Lil as she went through to the kitchen.

'Oh Mrs Richards watch my scones!' Lil was just opening the oven door.

'Oh sorry Lil, by the way have you seen George?'

'Well actually he was looking for you, something about that Inspector chap coming.'

'Oh I wonder what he wants this time' Rosemary looked a little put out. She was getting Simon his drink from the bar when George came in.

'A bit early for you isn't it?'

'This is for Simon, I'm getting him working for it mind you, I left him doing the flower bed.'

'Left him doing the flower bed, he can't tell a weed from a flower, he'll probably dig them all up! Oh by the way, Inspector Trafford called.'

'I know.' Lil said. 'What does he want?'

'He wants us all to have a meeting this evening, including Lil and Mary.'

'Well what if some of them are going out?'

'You will have to tell them to cancel whatever they are doing, he said it was important.'

'Maybe he's going to tell them that they can all go home. That will be welcome news, well except for Simon, he's depressed at the idea of going back.'

'Eight o'clock sharp he said. I'll go and tell Lil and Mary to stay behind tonight, you try and find the others.'

'Take this out to Simon will you?'

She handed him the drink and George went out.

✳ ✳ ✳

'I wonder if he's going to tell us who did the murders?' Sylvia sounded excited.

'I don't suppose he knows. Still, he might let us leave. I need to get back.' replied William.

'I thought you said the other day that work could wait?'

'Well, I can't stay away for ever and I need to get things moving with the solicitor about our separation.'

'Oh so you meant what you said, I thought perhaps you were going through the male menopause.'

'Of course I bloody meant it. The quicker we're shut of one another the better.'

'I couldn't agree more darling' Sylvia laughed as she flounced out of the room.

CHAPTER NINETEEN

The final countdown

The clock in the hall chimed. It was eight o'clock. Rosemary had arranged for the evening meal to be served earlier and had put some extra chairs in the lounge.

Lil had made some cheese straws and Rosemary had put a couple of bottles of sherry out. She was just putting extra ashtrays around the room when George came in.

'What's all this, it's not a party you know?'

'Well I spoke to the Inspector today and he said although it was an official visit, he said that he hoped the atmosphere would be as relaxed as possible.'

'Well I don't think he's got a cat in hells chance of that. I mean they are all under suspicion.'

Just then the doorbell rang.

'I'll get it' said George.

The Inspector and Sergeant Roper entered the

drawing room.

'I'll fetch them all in if you like' said Rosemary and she left the room.

Celia and Peter Bellamy entered the room first. Celia was asked by the Inspector about her health and she answered accordingly.

William, Simon followed and Mary started to hand the sherry around.

'I don't like sherry, can't we get something from the bar?' Simon moaned. Rosemary nudged him.

'Have this for now and shut up!' she said tensely.

'I hope this isn't going to take too long only my husband will be waiting for his tea.' said Lil.

Sylvia entered the room looking like a model. She was wearing a backless burgundy velvet dress.

'Good evening Inspector, sergeant, how nice to see you again' she smiled.

'Why the hell has she got that on?' thought Rosemary.

Sylvia was hoping that she would make the final grand entrance in her designer dress but Mavis foiled her plan by scurrying into the drawing room last, looking red and flushed apologising to the Inspector and everyone else.

When they were finally all seated the Inspector rose and walked into the middle of the room.

'I would like thank you all for being here, especially the staff as I know that you have had a long day and want to get home.'

Lil and Mary nodded in agreement.

'Don't we all?' said Peter.

'As you are aware there have been two recent deaths, both of the deceased we believe to be murder victims. Firstly the late Mrs Hounslow. As you probably know Dixogin tablets were put into her stomach medicine, so the murderer had to be pretty certain that she would need to take it, so she had to be made ill, not desperately ill but just enough for her to take her medicine. I believe a few drops of weed killer were put into her food on the night of her death. Since the starter the mussels in white wine sauce were the only thing to be left on the table and the main meal and the sweet were served at the table, it's more than likely that the weed killer was put into her starter.

Now the kitchen staff had every opportunity to tamper with the food.'

'Now look here' Lil got up from her seat.

'Please sit down Mrs Burridge. I said you had the opportunity. I didn't say that you used it. However, Mary you could have put something in Mrs Burridge's food to make her ill and it could have got into the guests by mistake.'

'What's this Mary, you wouldn't do such a thing!'

And you Mrs Burridge, you didn't like Martha Hounslow did you? You were heard quarreling with her one day.'

'She came into my kitchen and started questioning me about the way I cooked food. It was none of her business. What right had she, that's what I would like to know?'

'You despised her didn't you, because she had everything you've never had . . . money . . . position. She had an easy life?'

'Yes that's true. I've worked all my life even when my children were young. I've always had to. Yes, that woman had everything but she wasn't content always had to interfere and poke her nose in the running of the hotel and how I cooked the meals. It had nothing to do with her!'

'Ah well, that's where you are wrong. She had lent Mrs Richards money and she wanted to make sure that she got it back and if that meant making certain the hotel was run more efficiently then she would interfere.'

'Mother lent you money for the hotel? She never said anything to me about it. I can see now why she kept interferring, but why didn't she tell me?'

'Oh, so she didn't tell her precious son. I thought she confided every little detail to you.' Sylvia said rather pleased with herself.

'I had to borrow it, I was desperate.' Rosemary turned to William.

'Yes you were weren't you? You would have been devastated if you had have lost this place and Martha Hounslow could have caused you a lot of trouble, but there was no official agreement. With her out of the way the loan would have become void. She stood between you and this place.' The Inspector said.

'Well a friend was going to lend me the money to pay her back so I'd have been out of her debt.'

'Well that's what he says but we have checked his financial position and I don't think he had the funds to do such a thing.'

'Rubbish. He was going to to let me have the money.'

'Was he? Or did he just lie for you? Was you ever at his house that night before you went to Janet Morgans'

'He would not lie for you unless something was going on between you' George looked anxious.

Rosemary took his hand.

'Surely after twenty years of marriage you know me by now. I wouldn't do anything like that.'

'But would you kill Martha Hounslow to save this place for your wife George, and ordinary unromantic man some might say, but faced with this predicament . . . '

George never answered. The Inspector walked to the window.

'Now going back to when the starters were served, it was rather convenient the way everyone rushed outside to look at William's car.'

'Well the women were still in the dining room. Myself, Celia, Martha and Mavis. It was only the men who went out.' said Sylvia.

'Your car wasn't damaged by a vandal. We found a nail file with your car paint along the edge on you wife's dressing table. Your car was scratched deliberately to give someone the chance to mess with Mrs Hounslow's starter, unless of course one of the men dropped something into it on their way back in.'

'So you deliberately scratched my car, you bitch, how would you like it if I slashed one of your designer dresses?'

'I didn't scratch your bloody car, someone else did, they just used my nail file.'

'Martha Hounslow either knew something about someone or had a hold on them.' The Inspector turned to Peter Bellamy. 'I mean she knew about you're affair with Sylvia Hounslow and threatened to tell your wife. Surely you'd kill for that so that you wouldn't be exposed?'

'I didn't believe she would do it.' Peter replied.

'But she did, didn't she? She told you' the Inspector turned to Celia. Her eyes filled with tears.

'Yes. I couldn't believe it but I know now that she was telling the truth, I caught them in the garden.'

'Well you randy old sod!' Simon smiled at Peter.

Rosemary punched Simon on the arm.

'You had the baby on the way, everything in the garden was rosy. I think you always suspected your husband of being a bit of a flirt but you thought that when you were a family things would improve.'

'Yes I did, but Martha said that he had never be any good. She told me about all the women he'd had and she went into details it made me feel sick. Yes I hated her, I wanted to kill her. I thought she had made it up' Celia began to sob.

'You were in the dining room, you could have easily dropped the weed killer in her starter couldn't you?'

'Yes, I could have. I wish I had killed her. I wish that I had thought of the idea, but if I had I would have regretted it. Everything she said about my husband was true.'

'But darling, I love you. I mean they were just flings.' Peter jumped to his feet.

'She promised you didn't she that if you finished your fling with Sylvia Hounslow, she wouldn't tell your wife and you did finish it didn't you?'

'Yes. I realised the important thing was Celia and the baby and our life together. I'd have done anything to protect that.'

'Even murder?' the Sergeant asked.

'Even murder' Peter replied.

'She knew something about you too didn't she Mr Turley?'

'I don't know what you're talking about.'

'Fishing is an expensive hobby and you are not that well paid, we've checked up with your employer. Didn't you once do a job for a friend of Martha Hounslow and a considerable amount of money went missing?'

'It was never proven. It wasn't me, I knew nothing about it.'

'But she did. it wouldn't have gone down very well with your friends at the fishing club, especially since they had the club funds taken. That's one thing you love is your fishing. You wouldn't have wanted to be banned from the club and lose the respect that the men had for you.'

'But I wouldn't have killed the old cow. I hated the sight of her but I wouldn't have killed her.'

'Wouldn't you? Of course, she knew a lot about Dave Cranmore's business, but the fact that he too was murdered obviously excluded him. But he knew something about one of you in this room and he was blackmailing that person. The only one with any money is you Mr Hounslow.'

'Blackmailing me, what a ludicrous idea? He knew nothing about me.'

'You'll be a very rich man when your Mother's estate is settled, won't you Mr Hounslow?'

'I had plenty of money before.'

'You were comfortable then, but now if you invested wisely, you need never have to work again.'

'Yes, you are a lucky blighter. Thousands that's what you'll have, thousands and I only pinched a few hundred quid and I was being victimised.' Simon suddenly stopped realising what he had said.

'The idea that I would get rid of my own mother is unthinkable and I object to such an insinuation Inspector.'

'I believe you were fond of her, but you have always had money maybe you were fonder of that?'

'I won't stand for this. I'm leaving.' He got up to go. Sergeant Roper sat him back down and stood in front of the door.

'I haven't finished yet and you will stay until I have.'
He turned to Sylvia Hounslow. 'You will have a tidy
amount won't you even though you and Mr Hounslow
are divorcing?'

'How did you find that out you naughty man?' Sylvia
lit a cigarette.

'You hated her and she hated you didn't she?'

'That's absolutely correct, and you don't have to be a
good detective to work that one out. Yes I hated her and
if some clever bugger hadn't put the stuff in her
medicine, I'd have killed her. I was planning to.'

'I know you were' said the Inspector.

'Oh don't be silly Sylvia, you don't mean that, you're
just being melodramatic.' Mavis said.

'Oh yes I do . . . someone beat me to it, it is as simple
as that.'

Sergeant Roper stood up and looked around the
room.

'So what you are saying Sir is that anyone of these
people had a reason to kill her. Mr Hounslow for her
money, Mrs Hounslow also for money and also because
she disliked her. Mrs Richards because of the money
that Martha Hounslow had loaned her for the hotel.
Perhaps Mr Richards because he wanted to protect his
wife.'

'That's correct sergeant, but remember he said that
he didn't know about the loan until after her death.'

'I didn't!' George piped in.

'Then there is Mr Bellamy. What would he have done

to stop Martha Hounslow from telling his wife about the past? Although she did tell her but he wouldn't have known about that. When she did spill the beans to Mrs Bellamy she was horrified even though I suspect she may have exaggerated the truth a little. I suppose you didn't really want to know did you?' He turned to Celia?'

'No I didn't.' she said.

'Precisely. What the eye doesn't see, the heart doesn't grieve over. Then Mr Turley didn't want her saying anything about taking the money. so you see sergeant, you are quite right, all of them had a motive.'

'Well all except Mavis. She had no reason to kill my mother.'

'Ah but that's where you are wrong. She had the strongest motive of all of you.'

'Don't be bloody ridiculous. she couldn't hurt a fly. She hasn't got it in her.' Simon piped in.

'How would you know Mr Turley? The Inspector asked.

'How would I know? I've been married to the woman for twenty years.'Simon snapped.

'Yes and you probably know less about her than somebody who has been together a month. Do you know her likes, her dislikes, how she feels about things? Her strengths, her weaknesses? I think not Mr Turley because you never had the time or the inclination. I'm right aren't I Mrs Turley?'

Mavis nodded. Simon got up from his seat.

'It's a damn cheek. My married life is my own affair

and I cannot see what all this has to do with the murders. Hurry up and get this over with.

'Can't you Mr Turley? That's a pity because it's got everything to do with them.'

'What do you mean Inspector?' Rosemary asked anxiously.

'Well when the weed killer was put into Martha Hounslow's starter it had been done very quickly without anyone noticing. I believe it was dropped into the meal with an ear dropper like this one.' He reach into his pocket and produced a little glass phial with a rubber top. 'You could walk past the table it would only take a couple of seconds.' he demonstrated. 'You had an infected ear and were taking the drops weren't you Mrs Turley?'

'Yes but anyone could have taken it. Actually I couldn't find it for a couple of days.'

'Since the men were outside looking at the car that only left yourself, Sylvia and Celia in the dining room.'

'Well we didn't notice anything did we?' Celia asked Sylvia.

'Just think back for a moment. You were reading a book on pregnancy Mrs Bellamy?'

'Yes' she acquiesced.

'And were you engrossed in it?'

'Thinking back I was rather, I don't think I looked up.'

'And Mrs Turley gave you an article on Beauty care in a magazine to read' he turned to Sylvia. 'She knew that you spent a lot of time and money on yourself and that would have kept you occupied. finally Martha Hounslow was out on the terrace so you see, Mavis wouldn't have been noticed.'

William got to his feet.

'What you are saying is utterly ludicrous. I love Mavis, we intend to go away together. There is no reason on this earth why she would have murdered my mother.' he stepped towards the Inspector angrily.

Sergeant Roper came forward and asked him to sit down. Everyone looked shocked.

'You love Mavis and you intend to go away with her? Damn you William, are you bloody drunk or something?'

'I knew you'd say that Simon, you're a waste of time' William waved his hand at him in disgust. Simon started to take off his jacket.

'Let's sort this out man to man.'

'Sit down the pair of you and be quiet.' Sergeant Roper became rather forceful. 'Or I'll call for assistance.'

They both sat down grudgingly.

'We will sort this out later.' Simon said glaring at William.

'Now if I may continue. Thank you. You had scratched William's car with the nail file you had taken from Sylvia's room to make sure you got all the men out of the dining room.'

'But what about the Digoxin in the medicine . . .?' asked George.

'I'm coming to that. You work in a residential home

don't you Mrs Turley? Digoxin is a very common drug amongst the elderly as many of them have heart complaints. I'm sure it would be quite easy to remove some tablets from one of the residents rooms.'

'But what about Dave? Mavis would never kill Dave, she liked him.' said Sylvia amazed.

'Well Dave boasted that he knew something or had seen something. I'm not sure what, but she couldn't take the chance. Mavis arranged to meet him before she met you on Meadfoot beach Mr Hounslow.'

'But she arrived on time . . . '

'How did you know that she was on time? You hadn't got your watch on you. You had lost it! Rather a coincidence don't you think? Or perhaps Mrs Turley had taken it?'

'Well she came into my room to return a lipstick' said Sylvia. 'And it was about seven o'clock then.'

'How do you know?'

'She shouted the time to me, I was in the shower.'

'So you only had her word for that then hadn't you?' The Inspector turned to Mavis. 'I think you planned to murder Mr Cranmore even before you met him, that's why you disguised yourself in the wig and the glasses. Was he demanding money from you?'

'Well she had no money.' William said.

'No but she would have when she had married you. Maybe Dave would have settled for something on account, and the rest later when she became more affluent.'

'Well this is all well and good Inspector, but there's no motive. She wouldn't gain anything from mothers death, so all these assumptions are pointless.'

'But you would wouldn't you?' he turned almost kindly towards Mavis. The colour drained from her face. She looked sad like a small child.

'Tell them Mavis, for God's sake tell them it's not true.'

'I can't darling. Oh I love you so much but I can't. I killed your mother.'

There were gasps of shock and disbelief.

'No! You couldn't do such a thing. She could!' he angrily pointed at Sylvia. 'but not you, not you.' His voice became shaky.

'Would you like to tell us in your own words now Mrs Turley or you can give us a statement in private at the station?'

'I'll tell you now, it makes no odds.'

'Well in that case Mrs Turley, I am arresting you for the murder of Mrs Martha Hounslow and Mr David Cranmore. I must caution you that you are not obliged to say anything but anything you do say may be taken down in evidence and used against you in a Court of Law.' The Inspector looked solemnly at Mavis.

'Don't say a word Mavis, I'll get you a solicitor, the best money can buy' cried William.

'No, it's alright darling, I want to tell you.'

Sergeant Roper turned on the tape recorder. The room was silent.

213

'You were right what you said about my husband' Mavis began.

'He's never give a damn about me. My life with him has been one long drudge. He's never bothered with me or taken me anywhere. There's been no fun in our marriage, but what's worse is that there has never been any love. I've been deprived of that the last twenty years and we all need love to survive don't we?'

The Inspector nodded his head in agreement.

'I had reached forty, the crossroads in my life, the dreaded middle age and what had I done with my life? What had I achieved? Nothing. I had never known true happiness. Then you came along.'

She turned to William her voice becoming softer. 'You loved me and you could have given me a good life. I don't just mean money or possessions, those have never really been important to me because I have never really had them, but you talked about taking me abroad and on a cruise. I would have seen the world, experienced things that i had only dreamed of. I was still young enough to do all those things. It was a new lease of life for me, one last chance. But it wasn't just for the excitement or the fact you had the money to give me that sort of life. You had shown me what it was like to be truly loved. Love is something I thought I would never have.' She gazed at William longingly.

'But why mother, surely you didn't have to?'

'But I did. She said that we would never be able to be together, and she would do everything to stop us and she would have succeeded. She was a powerful woman, her personality was too strong and dominant. I knew I couldn't compete with her. She was going to take everything away from me. The last years of my life were going to be happy years with you, even though we would have had some opposition from Sylvia and Simon I could have coped with them easily.'

'I don't think so.' said Sylvia.

'Of course I could. You're just a silly, vain creature. As long as you had plenty of money to buy all your fancy clothes you'd have been okay. You would have found some other mug who would have put up with you.'

'And what about me?' Simon asked.

'What about you, whenever have you ever considered me? I didn't give a damn about you. I just wanted to get away and live my life. Oh I could have coped with you two.' She waved a finger at them. 'Martha was the problem. She was too strong. I knew she'd succeed in separating us, she wasn't going to ruin my chance of a wonderful life. I had to kill her, you see that don't you?' she pleaded with William. 'It was sad about Dave, I always liked him, but he had seen me go into Martha's room and he also hinted that he knew more. You were right Inspector, I didn't know exactly how much he had seen but I knew he wanted money. I'd got a thousand saved in the Building Society that I had been keeping for a rainy day. I'd have given him that but I knew that when William and I were together he would keep coming back for more. I would never have been free of him. I couldn't have had that hanging over our life together. You all know what Dave was like, he would have blown that thousand on some dicey business deal.' She lent on the mantlepiece. 'No, it was a pity about Dave but he had to go, you see that don't you?' She turned her head towards Inspector Trafford.

'Well I think that you had better come with us now Mrs Turley.'

'I can't Inspector. William and I have plans to make we're going away together.' Her voice sounded strange and a malevolent look came into her eyes. 'You understand Inspector, I can't go with you. I'm free of Martha and Dave now, I can go with the man I love and have a wonderful life.'

Simon walked towards her. 'Don't be so bloody stupid Mavis, you've got to go with the Inspector.'

In a split second she bent down and took a poker that was standing by the side of the fire and struck Simon across the head with such force that he staggered back and fell over.

The Inspector and Roper were by her side in a split second restraining her. They removed the poker from her hand.

Rosemary and Celia were bending down next to Simon, the blood was gushing from the wound all over the carpet.

'Ring for an ambulance quick.' Cried Rosemary.

Mavis began to scream hysterically. 'You see, you can't stop me, nobody can. This is my life and I'm going to enjoy it!'

Her screams could still be heard as Inspector Trafford, Roper and two police officers escorted her down the drive to the car.

CHAPTER TWENTY

Looking back

Inspector Trafford and Sergeant Roper were walking along Meadfoot beach.

'So you were wrong about her taking the Digoxin from the home.' said Sergeant Roper.

'Yes apparently she had no intentions of killing Martha Hounslow when they all arrived here. I should imagine that it was only after the confrontation when Martha said that she would stop her and William being together. Mrs Turley used to get all the prescriptions for the residents and she happened to have a repeat prescription of Digoxin in her bag.'

'Lucky for her you might say, or I suppose unlucky that she used it. So you think if she hadn't have had it she wouldn't have committed murder? asked Roper.

'I think she was so desperate to get rid of Mrs Hounslow that she would have found some other way. In her statement she had said she asked Dave to bend down to do her shoelace up and then she had hit him over the head with a hammer taken from the Richards' garden shed. As he fell forward, he had clawed at her tights and that is why he had particles of nylon beneath his nails.'

'Actually I do remember' said Roper 'Something Mr Hounslow said about her turning up that evening with a shopping bag. I suppose the wig, glasses and the hammer were in there. A bit risky don't you think?'

'Well yes possibly, but I suppose she had reckoned on William not wanting to know what was in the bag.'

'Well that hammer is a good piece of evidence with the hair and blood particles matching up to those of the victims. But why the hell did she give the wig and glasses and even the ear dropper to the charity shop, that was her biggest mistake? I don't understand.'

'Don't you Roper? She had never had anything. She'd had to scrimp and save all her life. She just couldn't bare to throw anything away. She thought they may have come in handy for someone.'

'Well they were certainly useful to us, but fancy using them to commit murder and then giving them away!'

'I know it sounds strange, but that's the way she was. She never wasted anything.'

✳ ✳ ✳

George and Rosemary had seen William and Sylvia

off earlier. William was adamant that they would still part despite what had happened.

George was sitting in the drawing room gazing out onto the front lawn.

'Well I won't be sad to see them go.'

Rosemary came up behind him and put her arms around his shoulders.

'I know, it will be nice to get back to normal. I really thought we could have lost everything you know. Simon made me realise how lucky we are.'

'I know, it's a turn up for the books him sticking to Mavis after all what's happened. He said that he will stand by her, through the trial. William said he just couldn't forgive her. He loved her, but was so close to his mother, he couldn't accept what she had done.'

'Poor Mavis. You know the day she arrived she was on about the sixties and her lost youth. If only I'd have known perhaps I could have prevented it.' she sighed.

'Oh Rosemary don't say that. There's nothing anyone could have done. Mind you, I think Peter's a changed man. He'll be more responsible now he's going to be a father.'

'Oh I don't know . . . a leopard never changes his spots.'

'You know your trouble Rosemary, you have no faith in the male population.'

They went out to see Celia and Peter off. George suggested that Celia sit in the back due her condition and began to help her in.

Rosemary was putting some bags on the front seat for Peter, as she bent over she felt someone pinch her bottom.

George and Rosemary waved to them as they drove away and began to walk up the driveway.

'No faith in the male population eh!' She smiled to herself.

THE END

THE END